# THE LONG

# SHADOW

# OF

# MEMORY

Nichole Heydenburg

Dedicated to Kate, aka "Box." I couldn't ask for a better sister or best friend. Love you forever.

# The Long Shadow of Memory

# Other Books by Nichole Heydenburg

*The Long Shadow on the Stage-*

Book 1 in *The Long Shadow Thriller Series*

# Chapter 1

He was laying on the side of the road with a duffel bag at his feet. He stood shakily and looked around, seeing single-story, traditional homes and palm trees lining the manicured lawns. The thick, humid air enveloped him. Where was he? He felt a sharp pang in his head and wondered what happened. He didn't know where he was or how he ended up here. The worst part was that he couldn't remember who he was, not even his name. In fact, the more he thought about it, the less he understood about his situation. He was in a strange place with no memories and no clues. Did he have amnesia? Was he near home? What happened to cause him to lose his memories? The only items inside the duffel bag were some clothes, toiletries, a worn paperback copy of short works by Edgar Allan Poe, and a photo of a man with short black hair, sparkling green eyes, and a nice smile. He didn't know who the man was, but he was attractive. As he pondered the situation, the throbbing in his head strengthened. He needed water and some food.

He wandered through the unfamiliar streets, seeing tanned people walk by, most of them wearing t-shirts and shorts with sandals. People avoided eye contact with him when he tried meeting their gaze to ask where he was, so he continued down the sidewalk for several blocks. The sun beat harshly down on him as he walked. Finally, he came across a restaurant with a glowing, neon sign out front that read Sofia's Cocina and Tequilería. It looked like a nice enough place to grab lunch, so he entered the restaurant. The hostess eyed him wearily when he approached and told him they were packed. He would have to wait over an hour for a table, unless he wanted to sit at the bar. The bar was fine with him.

He grabbed a stool at the bar, settling onto the vinyl leather seat, and looking around at the furnishings and decorations in the restaurant as he waited for the bartender to serve him. The walls were adorned with brightly colored landscape paintings and sombreros in a variety of shapes and sizes. A few minutes later, a tall, muscular man with spiky black hair and arms covered in tattoos approached him.

"Welcome to Sofia's Cocina and Tequilería. I'm the bartender, Liam. Do you want something to drink?"

He considered ordering wine, but thought water would be better for his aching head and parched lips. He was probably dehydrated.

"Water would be great, thanks. So…" The man paused, clearing his dry throat.

Liam appraised the man, looking concerned, and cut him off before he could continue. "Are you okay? Were you in an accident?"

The man paused. He was unsure how to respond because he didn't know what happened or how he looked. Was he in an accident?

Maybe that was why he couldn't remember anything. Maybe he had been injured and lost his memory from a concussion.

"Where are we?" The man asked, rubbing his aching head.

Liam stared at him, eyeing him suspiciously for a few seconds before answering. "You don't know where you are? What happened to you?"

"Can you please tell me where we are, so I can figure out where the hell I'm supposed to stay tonight?" The man asked, exasperated.

"Lake Chapala, Mexico," Liam responded, his placid smile wavering at the man's abrupt change in tone.

The man hesitated. "Lake Chapala?" He stumbled over pronouncing the unfamiliar name.

What the fuck was he doing in Mexico?

"Yup. Well, whatever happened, you can use the bathroom to clean up if you want," Liam suggested. "It's straight back there," he said, pointing.

*Fuck it. Nothing could possibly make my head hurt worse. I need a drink.*

"Sure, yeah, I'll be right back. Can I have a glass of red wine? Whatever you have is fine."

"Ah, a wine guy," Liam said, smiling. "Absolutely. I'll grab your wine while you're gone."

The man hoisted his duffel bag onto his shoulder and went to the bathroom. As he washed his hands, he timidly looked in the mirror to appraise his appearance. He needed to assess the damage. His long, dark hair looked stringy, like it hadn't been washed in weeks. His face was smudged in what appeared to be dirt and he had a cut on his head that no longer bled, but was scabbed over with dried blood. The cut explained the constant throbbing. A concussion seemed like a definite possibility. He turned on the water faucet again, this time turning it to the hottest setting, and shoved his head under the sink, scrubbing furiously with the cheap-smelling soap most restaurants have in their bathrooms.

He wrung out his long hair over the sink and dug in his duffel bag to see if he missed any items. There was a box of contacts at the bottom. That could explain the headache too. He popped in a new pair of contacts and changed his clothes, throwing the dirty, disheveled outfit into the trash can near the door.

When the man returned to the bar, Liam was serving another customer. He took a sip of his wine, savoring the taste. Well, he enjoyed red wine and now he knew his eyesight was terrible. It was a start.

Liam returned several minutes later. "Feel better? What did you do, shove your head in the sink?" He asked with a smirk.

The man's cheeks flushed. "Yeah, well, I kind of look like shit." He cleared his throat. "Can I order?"

"Sure, what do you want?"

"A chicken burrito, rice, and refried beans."

"Alright, I'll get your order in. How's the wine, by the way?" Liam asked.

"Great."

"I'm a beer guy, but I can respect that. Look, I know we just met and I'm only your bartender… But I moved here from the US a few years ago, so I know my way around Lake Chapala. It's where most expats end up. If you need a place to stay, The Sunset Motel is nice, well, for a motel. It's in a safe area."

His head throbbed violently. He wasn't sure if it was from drinking the glass of wine so fast without eating or his head injury or because his entire world had been flipped upside down. Not to mention the fact that he didn't even know what his normal world was like. "Okay," he finally blurted to Liam. He didn't relish the idea of accepting help from a stranger in a foreign country, but what choice did he have?

Liam rested his elbow on the bar counter and leaned closer to him. "What happened to you?" He asked softly, so no one else in the restaurant could hear.

"I don't know," the man said honestly. "I think I have amnesia."

"Are you serious?" Liam's eyes widened.

"Yeah, I can't remember anything. I don't know who I am or how I got here. I think I must have been…in some sort of accident." He paused, his head pulsing in pain as he concentrated on trying to remember any detail that could help him. "I wish I knew what happened to me."

Liam's face softened. "Okay, well after my shift ends this afternoon, I can take you over to The Sunset Motel. Whatever happened to you, at least you can stay there tonight and be safe in a warm bed."

"Thanks," the man said. "You don't have to do that though. I'm sure I can find a motel by myself."

Liam shrugged his shoulders. "I'm only trying to help. I know how hard it is to adjust to being in another country, so I can't imagine how much more difficult it is when you've lost your memory."

The man looked down at his empty wine glass. "Can I have another glass of wine?"

A smile tugged at the corner of Liam's thin lips. "Do you want to try the local tequila instead? It's made nearby in Jalisco."

The man paused, wondering if he enjoyed tequila or if he would be able to hold it down. "Sure, why not?"

Liam laughed. "That's the spirit! While you're in Mexico, embrace the culture." He poured a small amount into a glass and added grapefruit soda. "Traditionally, you drink it in a snifter and slowly sip it to savor the taste, but some people mix it with grapefruit soda if they don't want to drink it straight."

The man slowly picked up the glass after Liam placed it in front of him. He carefully sniffed the drink before taking a cautious sip. Liam chuckled at the shock on the man's face.

"Well, I don't think it would be my first choice," the man said, taking another dainty sip of the tequila and grapefruit soda cocktail, "But it's better than I expected."

"I'm glad you like it," Liam said, looking around the bar to make sure there weren't any customers waiting to be served. "Thankfully, you stumbled in here as the lunch rush died down, so you'll probably be my only customer for a bit."

"How long have you worked here?" The man asked Liam.

"A few years. I don't have many talents, but I would like to think I'm skilled at making drinks and personable enough to be a bartender," he said, smiling playfully. "Plus, I meet tons of cute guys."

The man felt his cheeks redden and hastily took another sip of his cocktail. "Yeah, well, I'm sure that's a perk."

"Let me go check on your food," Liam said, rushing off to the kitchen.

He thought about the photo stashed away in his duffel bag of the handsome man with the short black hair and green eyes. Was he his friend? Husband? Lover? The questions were piling up and he began to feel overwhelmed at the impossibility of answering all of them.

Liam returned a few minutes later with a plate stacked full with a chicken burrito and a heaping pile of rice and refried beans. "Enjoy."

"Thanks." The man picked up the chicken burrito and took a bite, his stomach suddenly growling. He wondered when he had last eaten. He quickly finished the burrito and moved onto the rice and beans, scraping the rest of the food off the plate with his fork so he could eat every bite.

Liam returned to the kitchen to check on another order. The man pondered his situation. He cautiously considered every angle of Liam's offer to show him The Sunset Motel. But what if Liam was a criminal? Maybe he was involved in sex trafficking. Or he could be a drug dealer. He barely knew him, so was it wise to trust someone he had known for less than an hour? Besides, why was Liam being so nice to him?

Liam came back to see if the man liked his meal, but was surprised to find the plate cleared. "I guess you won't be wanting a takeout container then."

"No, but the check would be great, thanks."

"You got it."

The man suddenly felt woozy, perhaps from drinking a glass of wine and a tequila cocktail on an empty stomach, then shoveling down an enormous amount of food in record time. He was unsure what his usual alcohol intake was, so he didn't know if he was a lightweight and merely at his limit.

Liam came back with the check. "There you go." He hesitated, fiddling with an empty glass on the bar counter. "Look, I know you weren't thrilled about my offer to escort you to the motel, but the offer still stands. My shift is over soon if you don't mind waiting."

The man checked his back pocket for his wallet, but it wasn't there. He stood up, reaching his hand into every pocket and coming up empty handed. "Shit."

He opened his duffel bag and searched each pocket and compartment inside, looking for a wallet, a credit card, or cash. Unfortunately, there wasn't any form of currency inside his bag.

Liam watched the man helplessly search through his belongings and realized the issue. "You don't have any money, do you?"

The man stood from where he had been crouching over his duffel bag and ran his hands through his long, semi-dried hair. "No, I guess not. I should have double checked before I ordered. It was stupid of me to assume…"

"Okay, so you ordered two drinks and a meal, but you have no way to pay for it, right?" Liam asked.

"No, I don't. Unless you want this beaten-up copy of Edgar Allan Poe short stories," the man said with a grimace.

"Sorry, we don't barter for meals here," Liam chortled. "I get a free meal with my shift every day, but I didn't eat one today, so the food is taken care of. The drinks, on the other hand…"

The man slumped onto the barstool. "So, I have nowhere to stay, no money, and now I have no way to pay for my drinks. This situation keeps getting better."

"I'll cover your drinks, but what are you going to do afterwards?" Liam said.

"Are you sure?"

"Yeah, don't worry about it."

"And I suppose you're right. I need money, so I should find a job," the man responded dejectedly.

"I could use some help here, especially on weekends. I can talk to the restaurant manager and see if he would be willing to hire you. Miguel is a great guy; he took a chance on me when I moved here."

"Yeah, okay. That's not a bad idea."

"I'll go talk to Miguel and see what he thinks, but I'm sure he will go for it."

"Thanks, Liam," the man said, looking directly into Liam's eyes for the first time since he met him.

Liam smiled. "You're welcome. I believe you get back what you put out into the world, so I always try to help people when I can."

"I like that philosophy. It sounds like a good way to live."

Liam walked away to talk to Miguel. The man pondered his situation once more, his anxiety growing by the minute. What if Miguel wouldn't hire him? Then what would he do? Would they call the police and have him arrested? What would happen if he was stuck in prison with no memories, no one to call for help, no bail money, and no way home? Hell, he didn't even know where home was.

"Good news…uh, I just realized I don't even know your name," Liam said.

"Oh. Right. Like I said earlier I think I have amnesia… I don't remember anything. Not even my name."

"Huh. What a predicament. Well, you need a name. What about Klaus?"

"Klaus?" The man asked with a frown. "I don't think so."

"Sorry, that was random. I re-watched *The Originals* recently and it was the first male name that popped into my head."

"I don't know what that is, but do you have any other ideas?"

"Oh! We will have to watch it together sometime. It's the best modern day vampire show." Liam paused for a minute in concentration as he ran through a list of every male name he could think of off the top of his head. "What about…Kevin?"

"Kevin? Hmm, maybe."

"Or Ted. Like Ted Bundy, the serial killer. I love true crime shows and movies. I've watched every documentary and movie about Ted Bundy."

"A serial killer?" The man said, his eyes widening.

"Yup. He targeted young women and got away with it for years until he was finally caught. He ended up confessing to 30 murders, but there could have been more."

"Wow…"

"Not Ted then?"

"No. I think Kevin is fine," the man said, wondering how someone could kill 30 people. Did he kill them all the same way or did he switch it up sometimes? How would you even begin to get away with that?

# Chapter 2: Delia

Delia Wilson finished another shift at The Fox Luxury Apartments where she worked as a security officer and headed home. She wanted a less dangerous job after what happened last winter. Not that she felt any safer now. She took a pay cut with her new job, which meant she could no longer afford to live in Manhattan. Now Delia lived in Queens, despite the hour-long commute.

The months dragged by, but it was already spring. In NYC, this meant there was slushy, dirty snow in the streets and she still had to scrape the ice off her car every morning and allow extra time for her car to heat up before driving to work. But it would be warmer soon and Delia hoped as spring turned to summer and the months continued to pass, she would forgive herself for letting him get away with the murders.

She knew it was silly, but as she left the liquor store and crossed the street to return to her car, she thought she saw him. She recognized the eyes immediately. Those haunting dark brown eyes that bore into her soul. They were such a dark brown they almost looked black. Delia was filled with an eerie sense that he knew her every thought and every move. She hesitantly stepped closer to the man, not because she wanted to, but rather she felt pulled toward him. She needed to know if it was him.

As the man with the dark eyes noticed her moving uncomfortably close to him, he reached out his hand in a stopping motion and said, "Sorry, ma'am, can I help you? Do I know you from somewhere?" In a thick New York accent.

She looked into his eyes again after hearing him speak and saw that his eyes were brown, but a soft brown, kind, welcoming—not the eyes of a killer. "Oh, um, no. Sorry! I thought you were someone else." Delia quickly started to walk away.

"Are you sure you're okay?" The man called out. "Do you need help with those bags?" He asked, gesturing to the two large, brown paper bags full of liquor nestled tightly into her arms.

Delia blushed, embarrassed about the amount of liquor in her bags. "No thanks, I can manage." She paused. "It's not all for me. It's for a party," she explained.

The man waved her off, chuckling. "I'm not judging you, don't worry. Enjoy your night."

"You too," she replied, unlocking her car with the key fob and placing the bags carefully in the backseat of her Honda Civic.

Delia drove home and started to unload her stockpile of liquor in her nondescript apartment with plain white walls and no wall furnishings. The walls weren't painted or patched, so there were still nails and marks on them from where the previous renters hung family pictures, framed canvases, pictures of the places they traveled, or whatever families hung on walls. She liked to think her apartment had a minimalist vibe, but in truth she didn't know shit about decorating. She also didn't care because there were only a handful of people who would ever see her apartment. Her best friend, Becca, reprimanded her plenty of times for not "embracing her creative side," which probably meant she wanted to decorate Delia's place herself. Delia didn't have a creative side, unless you counted letting her imagination run wild, constantly thinking the murderer that she let escape was still after her and wanted revenge.

Her dog, a lovable, hyperactive puggle with light brown fur named Lily, ran towards her as soon as Delia entered the apartment, greeting her by jumping on her and nearly knocking the bags out of her arms. Lily only weighed twenty pounds, so she was the perfect sized dog for living in an apartment, but she could be a bit much at times.

"Lily, stop! Calm down. I know I've been gone all day, but I'm home now."

Delia reached down to pet Lily, filled her food and water dishes, and ordered a pizza online. Lily seemed satisfied that Delia was properly greeted and wandered back to her plush dog bed in the living room.

Delia opened the first liquor bottle, Lunazul tequila, and poured a hefty amount into a glass, adding a splash of lemonade and a few ice cubes. It wasn't fancy or sophisticated, but it was cheap and after a few of these, she would be down for the night. She settled into the worn black leather couch and turned on the TV. Several minutes later, the doorbell rang with her pizza delivery. There was no better pizza in the world than authentic New York style pizza. At least, that was what any proud New Yorker would insist.

Delia spent the rest of the night eating pizza, drinking tequila, and watching TV while Lily snoozed contentedly near her feet. She didn't know what she was watching, but keeping the TV on helped her pretend she wasn't alone.

***

The next day, Delia had another long shift ahead of her. She woke up with the sensation that her head was slammed into a ton of bricks. She might have drunk one too many tequila and lemonade combos last night. Lily barked at her as she dragged herself out of bed and wearily tried to prepare herself for work.

During her shift at work, her boss, Will Bell, approached her. Will had cropped, black hair, and dark brown skin. He was a good boss. Probably the best boss Delia ever had. He cared greatly about his employees and wanted to see them all succeed.

"Delia, I think you should take a day off," Will said, leaning against the front desk where Delia was stationed. "When's the last time you took a vacation? I don't think you have since you started working here. You work too much."

Delia half-smiled, not able to muster up the energy for a full smile. "I appreciate the offer, Will, but I like staying busy with work. Besides, I don't need a vacation. There's nowhere for me to go. I'm perfectly fine staying in the city and working."

Will sighed and ran his hands through his short black hair. "I know you say that now, but you're still young. If you spend all your time working for the next ten, fifteen, twenty years, you'll be too old to enjoy your life by then. I insist you take tomorrow off and do something fun. Go out for lunch with Becca or take your weird little puggle to a dog park. Go outside and be around people."

"I'm around people plenty," Delia responded. "I'm talking to you right now, aren't I?"

Will chuckled and shook his head. "You're so stubborn. If you show up here tomorrow, I'm locking the door and turning you away."

At this statement, Delia laughed. "Will, I have keys to all the buildings. But I see your point. I'll call Becca and see if she's free tomorrow. But I'm only doing this because you're being so insistent."

"Do it for yourself. You deserve it. After what you went through last winter…" Will trailed off, breaking eye contact with Delia, aware he might be crossing a line. "I hope I'm not overstepping here, but you can't beat yourself up over what happened forever. Look, you're a great worker and you know how much I appreciate you always picking up extra shifts, but it seems to me you're letting what happened consume your life. You don't always have control over what happens, so don't dwell on the past. Forgive yourself for your mistakes. Don't forget to live."

Delia exhaled loudly, attempting to stay calm despite the mounting anxiety that threatened to overwhelm her every time she thought about her failure with her last case as a police officer. She let out a halfhearted laugh. "Fine, I get it. And you're wrong; I've forgiven myself and moved on."

Delia suspected Will knew she was lying, but he also knew it was pointless to try to discuss the subject further, especially with the mood she seemed to be in. It was best to let it be.

# Chapter 3: Kevin

Kevin stayed at The Sunset Motel as Liam suggested. The owner of the motel, Tony, seemed suspicious of Kevin when he explained his situation and his lack of a driver's license or any form of ID. However, Tony let him stay at the motel when Kevin offered to pay in cash. Miguel hired Kevin as a server at Sofia's Cocina and Tequilería and paid him after his first shift, so he could afford the motel. Kevin knew he needed to earn money while he tried to figure out his next move. He tried his best to adjust to his new life, but still constantly wondered how he ended up in Mexico and what happened to make him lose his memories. He researched amnesia and learned that head injuries could cause people to lose their memories. Liam had been a steady presence throughout the stressful week. It had only been a few days since they met, but Kevin knew he could trust Liam. Well, almost. It was hard to trust anyone when you didn't even know who you were.

Kevin sat on the bed in his motel room, waiting for Liam to pick him up. They had developed a routine together. Liam would swing by the motel, they would work together at the restaurant with Liam training him, then afterwards they would go out to eat or grab takeout from somewhere nearby. It was nice having someone to talk to, even if Kevin didn't want to talk much yet.

Kevin flipped through the channels on the TV as he waited for Liam. He stopped at random and aimlessly stared at the TV. Suddenly, he felt dizzy and flushed. A scene played through his mind like a movie. He sat on the ground, cradling the body of a man in his arms. There was a gun near him on the floor. The man's head bled freely and the blood flowed steadily onto Kevin's shirt. Kevin sobbed and held the man's lifeless body, rocking back and forth in vain.

Kevin jumped up from the bed and turned off the TV, rummaging through the motel room to find his duffel bag and the photo of the handsome man with the short black hair, tanned skin, and green eyes. Kevin stared at the photo, comparing it to the man he imagined in what he could only assume was a memory. It was the first memory to surface, so it must be important. Who was the man? Was he dead? And most importantly, how did he die?

Kevin contemplated these questions until Liam knocked on the door of his motel room. He wondered if he should tell Liam what he remembered. Maybe he could help him try to piece the jumbled mess together. On the other hand, what if the man died under suspicious circumstances? After all, Kevin wasn't sure how he lost his memories and the man he had remembered was probably dead. Maybe he should keep it to himself. Just in case.

# Chapter 4: Delia

Delia planned to meet her best friend, Becca, for lunch at one of their favorite cafés. When you live in a bustling city with expensive rent, small cafés come and go, but this one had stuck around for years. The inside was cozy; bright artwork of Paris landscapes adorned the pastel-colored walls, tiny circular tables posed for dining, plush velvet-lined chairs stood invitingly, and a giant stone fireplace took up one of the walls. The owners were an elderly couple who still ran the café and probably would until they died. Their café was known for its pastries and sandwiches, simple but delicately delightful food, and an assortment of teas and coffee from around the world which could be purchased at the shop in the adjoining room.

Delia wanted to rush out the door so she would arrive at the café early, but her mom had still been sleeping and she wanted to make sure her mom knew she would be gone for the day.

"Mom!" Delia called again, knocking on the door of the guest bedroom in her apartment for the third time and finally deciding to barge inside.

"Yes?" Her mom asked, peering at Delia over her black-framed, rectangular glasses. She was sitting in bed and holding a paperback book in her hands.

Delia stared at her, astounded. "Why didn't you answer when I kept knocking on the door?"

"Well, I figured you would give up and leave me alone eventually," her mom replied.

Delia shook her head in frustration. "I'm meeting Becca for lunch, then running some errands. I'll be back later." Delia paused in the doorway. "Will you be okay?"

"Delia, I'll be fine. Stop worrying about me," her mom said, opening the book and going back to reading.

"Okay. Text me if you need anything."

Delia left the apartment in a frenzy and still arrived at the café ten minutes early. She sat at one of the tables near the front entrance of the café, so she could look through the glass window into the street. She met Becca in high school. Becca married her high school sweetheart, Joel, and often invited Delia to be the third wheel on their dates. Becca was a best-selling novelist of a murder mystery series, so she frequently asked Delia for insight on criminal investigations and police procedures.

"Sorry, I'm late," Becca said, throwing down her large, red purse and breathing heavily. "I couldn't find a parking spot close by, so I parked four blocks away and walked here." Becca tousled her hair, which rested slightly above her shoulders and was currently dark blue.

Delia grinned at Becca and handed her a menu. "Trust me, if you were ever on time, I would probably question everything about our friendship. I like the blue."

"Thanks. I was sick of red. I might try pink next."

"How's the new book going?"

Becca absentmindedly glanced at the familiar menu, which was only one page front and back and hadn't changed since the café opened years ago. "It's fine. I'm sending it to my editor next month, so hopefully I can publish it this year. I'm trying to figure out what to do next because it's the last book in the series. Joel thinks I should start writing a new series, but I don't know. A break might be nice."

"A break from writing?" Delia asked, her eyes widening. For as long as she knew Becca, she had always been writing. Delia envied that Becca's chosen career was her passion, something she could devote her life to.

"Yeah, it wouldn't be a long break. I've been working so hard the past few years to finish this series and I'm getting burned out."

"You push yourself too hard sometimes. You should take a day off occasionally," Delia suggested.

Becca snorted. "Yeah, okay. Says the woman who hasn't taken a day off in months."

Delia fidgeted in her seat. "I took today off, didn't I?"

"Maybe we should go on a trip together. A girl's trip to Charleston or Savannah. Somewhere warm."

Delia laughed heartily. "I'm sure Joel would love that."

"He wouldn't mind having a few days alone. He can play video games and drink beer with his friends. He would love it. Besides, a getaway sounds perfect! We deserve it," Becca said, setting down the menu after finally making up her mind about her order.

The server came over to take their orders. Delia and Becca decided to share a pot of cranberry tea. Delia ordered a chicken, pesto panini with a side salad, while Becca ordered a chicken salad croissant.

"How's your Mom?" Becca asked, after a few moments of the two women eating their lunches in silence.

"She's…well…she's not doing great. I took her to see the doctor last week and she's been diagnosed with Alzheimer's. She's becoming very forgetful and was involved in several fender benders, which isn't like her at all, so I've been worried. The doctor said her mind is deteriorating rapidly. Some people can live with Alzheimer's for years, but I don't know how long she has left." Delia set her half-eaten panini back on the plate as a few tears slid down her cheeks.

"Delia, I'm so sorry," Becca said, standing from her seat and walking around to Delia's side of the table to hug her. "Your Mom has always been so wonderful to me. I'm sorry this is happening. But I'll be here for you through it all. Whatever you need, let me know. Okay?"

"Thanks, Becca, I appreciate it. But what I need right now is the money to afford a nice assisted living facility for my mom. I don't want to do it, but it's the best option. She's been living with me for a few days, but I can't take care of her. Since my dad has been gone for years and I don't have any siblings, the responsibility is on me."

"That must be really tough. If Joel and I weren't trying to fix up the house right now, you know I would help you with the money. I wish I could."

"It's fine. I wouldn't expect you to help me with this. Besides, I'm sure I'll figure something out."

Becca smiled warmly at her best friend. "I know you will. You always do."

***

Several hours later, Delia returned to her apartment after spending the day running errands. After the latest incident, her mom had temporarily moved in with her, so she needed to buy groceries and pick up her mom's newest medications. Delia always struggled to take a day off to relax and found herself busier than ever since her mom's diagnosis.

"There you are," a husky, deep voice suddenly said much too close to her.

"Oh!" Delia squealed, jumping back from the stranger and nearly dropping her groceries in the street.

"I've been waiting for you to come home. You're not an easy woman to find," the man said, brushing his shoulder length blond hair away from his ocean blue eyes. "It took me awhile to figure out where you lived, then even longer to track down where you're currently working, your license plate number…"

Delia cut him off. "Who are you? I'm a former police officer, so you should be careful what your next move is because I still have contacts at the NYPD 19th Precinct."

Delia immediately appraised the situation, scanning the man's frame for weapons. A gun partially stuck out of his hoodie pocket. She knew it was best to remain calm, stay alert, and try to talk him down without either of them becoming injured.

The blond-haired man laughed mockingly. "Of course you do. I know all about you, Delia. All about how you used to be a police officer, until you fucked up the last case you were on and ruined my life."

"Sorry. What case?" Delia asked, feigning confusion, unsure how this man was connected to Jackson and Clara's murders. Maybe he had been a friend of theirs or a relative?

"Don't play dumb with me. You know it's your fault Clara is dead. You should have protected her!" He screamed in anguish.

"Okay. Please take a breath so we can talk about this rationally. What's your name?"

The man huffed loudly, presumably trying to calm himself. "Blaine," he said, exhaling slowly.

"Okay, Blaine. How did you know Jackson and Clara?"

Blaine scoffed. "I don't care about Jackson. I only met Jackson once. I assume he didn't want Clara around me because he knew what would happen if we were alone together."

Delia paused, contemplating his connection. "How did you know Clara?"

"It doesn't matter how I knew her! The point is she's gone. I lost her and it's your fault," Blaine said angrily, moving closer to Delia.

"I understand why you would be upset. I did my best to protect both Jackson and Clara. Unfortunately, life doesn't always turn out the way we want it to, no matter how hard we try," Delia said solemnly. "I promise I did everything in my power to keep them both safe after Jackson was kidnapped. I didn't want any of this to happen. I live with the guilt of their deaths every day."

Blaine sneered. "You deserve the guilt after what happened to Clara. I still can't believe they closed the case, even though the murderer was never caught! Clara didn't commit suicide! If you knew her like I did, you would understand how she thought. Clara never would have wanted to kill herself. She wasn't depressed. She was grieving, but she was…falling in love with me."

Delia's face softened at Blaine's obvious grief. "I'm sorry you lost her, Blaine. But I do agree with you. I don't believe Clara committed suicide either. I'm not a police officer anymore. One of the reasons I quit was because of that case. The police chief, other investigating officers, and everyone else involved with the case thought Clara's confessional suicide note wrapped the case up neatly, so they were willing to close the case and move on. Meanwhile, the real murderer is still out there."

Blaine stared at Delia for a minute, considering his next move. "I don't believe you. As a former police officer, I'm sure you're quite skilled at manipulating people and talking them down from a ledge. But I'm not falling for it." Blaine pulled out the gun from his hoodie pocket. "This conversation has been fun, but I think it's time to end it."

Delia immediately reacted, unholstering her own gun and releasing the safety expertly within seconds. "Blaine, be very careful what you do next."

"I'm done being careful. I'm sick of feeling like this," Blaine said through clenched teeth. He raised the gun and held it with shaking hands, trying to aim at Delia's head.

Unfortunately for Blaine, Delia's steady hand came from years as a skilled former police officer. She fired her gun into the air, not aiming for Blaine, only trying to scare him. She didn't think he would shoot her, but she didn't want another innocent death on her hands, either.

Blaine jumped back when Delia's gun went off and dropped his own gun in shock. He fell to the concrete pavement, sobbing hysterically, holding his blond head in his hands. "I'm sorry, Clara," he muttered softly. "I tried to avenge you, but I wasn't strong enough. I was never strong enough for you."

Delia walked over to Blaine and picked up the gun, not wanting to take the chance that Blaine would change his mind about trying to kill her. "Blaine, are you okay?" She asked with trepidation.

"No…" He howled in sadness.

"Do you have someone you can talk to? A friend or a family member who can come over and stay with you tonight?" Delia asked.

"No, Clara was all I had. She was my friend and my true love. I know we would have ended up together if we had the chance."

"Okay. Well, I think we should go down to the police station and sort this out. We will need to file a police report," Delia said, kindly.

Blaine suddenly stood in panic. "The police station? Am I going to be arrested?"

"I won't press any charges, but you did stalk me and assault me with the intent, I'm assuming, of killing me."

"Please don't make me go there. It would ruin my life."

Delia sighed, not wanting to let him go, but at the same time wondering what the point would be to file a police report and force him to go to the station. She knew this urge came from her routine protocol knowledge, but she wasn't a police officer anymore. She didn't have an obligation to report the attempted assault.

"Fine. Go home and get some rest. I'm keeping this though," Delia said, tightly gripping both her own gun and Blaine's gun.

"Oh. Okay. Sorry about…" Blaine drifted off in a soft voice. Blaine started to walk away but turned around again to ask Delia a final question. "Delia, I know I don't have the right to ask you this, especially after I tried to harm you, but I would appreciate your help. You seem like a decent person and I know you're no longer a police officer, but you have the skills required for this sort of thing and I clearly don't. Will you track him down and find him? The guy who did it? Please? Will you find the guy who killed Clara and make him pay?"

Delia swallowed hard and nodded. "Okay, I'll find Edgar," she said, letting the name slip out.

Blaine leaned forward eagerly and Delia took a step back. "Is that his name? Edgar? Do you know where he is?"

"I'm not sure where he is, but I'll try to find out where he could have gone."

Blaine smiled gratefully, wiping his tear-streaked cheeks and shakily heading towards his car. "Thank you," he said over his shoulder as he walked away.

Delia sighed. What was she getting herself into?

# Chapter 5: Kevin

Kevin tried to be cautious with the money he earned from bartending. Miguel paid him in cash, so it was easy to keep track of his finances, although he realized he needed a better place than a duffel bag to stash his savings. At some point, if he regained his memory, he suspected he would want to go home. Wherever home was. If he stayed in Mexico for more than a few months, he would need to apply for a travel visa, but considering he didn't have a passport or any form of ID, he needed to leave the country before then.

He flipped through the tattered copy of Edgar Allan Poe short stories he found in his duffel bag. The cover page had a dedication clearly printed:

Edgar,

Happy 11th Birthday!

We hope you enjoy these dark tales from your namesake and that you appreciate them as much as we do.

With Love,

Mom and Dad


It was the first helpful clue he found, other than the "memory" that he wasn't sure was real. He could safely assume the book was his since it was with his small pile of belongings. Now he knew his name was Edgar and his parents were at least partially crazy if they named him after Edgar Allan Poe. Maybe they were writers too. Or literature professors. Or maybe they simply enjoyed creepy stories. Whatever the case, it wasn't enough to find out who his parents were or where he was from. At least he wouldn't have to go by Kevin anymore, which never felt right in the first place.

Liam had helped him purchase a cellphone, so he quickly Googled "Edgar Allan Poe" to find out more information about him. He felt a twinge of familiarity as he browsed through several articles describing the details of Poe's life and death.

When Liam took him shopping, Edgar also purchased several thrifty outfits, plus essential toiletries and snacks. He was trying to survive with the bare minimum so he could easily flee if necessary. After the memory of the man lying on him bleeding to death, he couldn't shake the feeling that he committed a terrible act. Somehow, he felt responsible for the mysterious man's death. He wanted to be ready if the authorities came for him.

Edgar didn't remember reading the book of short stories, so he spent his free time reading it from cover to cover. He was surprised to find many of the pages had highlighted passages and notes scrawled in the margins. He perused the notes and passages, interested in the musings of who he referred to in his mind as "Edgar 1.0." What was

Edgar 1.0 thinking when he read the collection of short stories? It was apparent the book was well-loved and had been read many times.

Edgar sat cross-legged on the lumpy motel bed, perusing the short story "The Tell-Tale Heart." The story disturbed him, but he loved how Poe personified the man's guilt in the beating heart he imagined hearing under the floorboards. A knock on the door disturbed Edgar from his literature analysis and he jumped off the bed to check the peephole on the door. He wasn't paranoid. He was simply being cautious. But it was only Liam.

Edgar opened the door to find Liam dressed in a nice, charcoal-colored button-up shirt with black dress pants. His hair was styled expertly, gelled over to the right side. He held a garment bag draped over his arms and smiled widely.

"What is that?" Edgar asked pointedly.

"Your outfit for our date tonight," Liam said, smiling even more.

"Our…what?" Edgar said, his face turning the reddest shade humanly possible.

"Yup. I'm taking you out. So put this on and we can go!"

Edgar sighed, picked up the outfit Liam handed him, and carried it into the bathroom. Liam knew his size since they shopped together earlier in the week. Edgar pulled out the outfit. It was a maroon button-up shirt and dark gray dress pants. After he put on the clothes, he looked at himself in the bathroom mirror. The shirt fit fine, but the pants were a little baggy, especially in the butt. He walked out of the bathroom, not feeling especially confident about how he looked.

"Wow! You look great all dressed up," Liam said, standing from the wooden chair where he had been sitting and appraising Edgar.

Edgar looked down at his baggy pants uncomfortably. "Are you sure?"

"You look good. I promise," Liam said, lightly brushing his hand against Edgar's shoulder comfortingly.

"If you say so. Where are we going on our date?"

"It's a surprise, but I think you're going to love it!" Liam said, smiling dazzlingly and grabbing Edgar's hand. "Come on, let's go. We have a reservation."

Liam tugged Edgar gently out the door and to his car. He drove a black Dodge Challenger and prized his car more than any of his possessions. He opened the passenger door for Edgar and walked around the car to slide into the driver's seat. "Buckle up, Kevin. It's going to be a night you'll never forget."

"Oh. Right." Edgar buckled his seatbelt. "My name isn't Kevin," he said quietly. "It's Edgar."

"How did you find out?" Liam asked, avoiding eye contact with Edgar and pulling out of The Sunset Motel's parking lot.

"I have a book of short stories and poems by Edgar Allan Poe in my duffel bag. On the cover page, there's an inscription from my parents. I guess they named me after Poe."

"Wow, that's crazy," Liam said, keeping his eyes focused on the road. "I mean, that's great you found out what your real name is, but…wow. What kind of parents name their kid after Edgar Allan Poe?"

"Yeah, I'm not sure how to feel about it. I wish there was a way I could find out more. I wish I could trigger my memories…"

"If I can help, let me know. I'll be there for you every step of the way, no matter what happens," Liam said. "But tonight, let's have fun."

***

Liam took him to a nice restaurant near Lake Chapala, then on a tour of a tequila distillery. Their last stop of the night was at a restaurant known for its tres leches cake. Liam made a reservation for a table on the rooftop, so they could stare out into the beautiful Lake Chapala, watch the people hurrying around the city, and enjoy the view of the twinkling night sky. Edgar didn't want the night to end, but as they were finishing their dessert, he started to wonder what Liam's expectations were after the date. He began to panic, thinking about what Liam wanted from him. He still didn't know much about Liam and decided he would have to be more careful going forward. He couldn't let his guard down.

A young couple sat at one of the rooftop tables across from them. While in deep thought, Edgar hadn't noticed they kept staring at him and whispering to each other, but Liam noticed. Liam jumped up from his seat, grabbing Edgar's hand and pulling him to his feet.

"Are you done with dessert?" Liam asked.

Edgar nodded and tucked his long dark hair behind his ears anxiously.

The young couple approached them. "Oh my God, I told you it was him!" The young woman said to her husband. "Sorry to bother you while you're out, but when I realized it was you, I wanted to come over to say hi."

Edgar stared at the young woman and man in confusion. "Sorry? Do I know you?"

The woman looked at her husband and giggled. "No, sorry if this is weird for you. I'm sure people approach you all the time. We love *Dispatching David*. We're huge fans and would appreciate it so much if we could get your autograph."

"My autograph? Why?" Edgar asked, looking at Liam for reassurance. Liam held tightly to his hand and tried to pull him away from the young couple.

"Come on, Edgar. Let's go," Liam said forcefully.

Edgar looked helplessly at the couple and smiled gently as Liam yanked him towards the exit door on the rooftop.

"What was that about?" Edgar asked Liam as they approached Liam's car.

"Nothing. It doesn't matter. Get in the car."

Edgar stood next to the car, refusing to open the door. His anxiety about Liam grew stronger by the minute. He wanted answers.

"Why did that couple act like they knew me? They said they love *Dispatching David*. What is that?" Edgar rapid fired the questions, realization dawning as he began to suspect the truth. "Did you recognize me when we first met? Do you know who I am?"

Liam leaned against the car and sighed. "Please don't be upset with me. Yes, I recognized you. At first, I assumed you were in some sort of disguise and didn't want people to know you were in Mexico. I didn't blame you. I'm sure it's hard for you to go anywhere without someone recognizing you from the show. But, after talking to you at the restaurant and hearing your story, I realized you had no idea you were Edgar Peterson, star of the popular detective show, *Dispatching David*."

"I'm an actor?" was all Edgar managed to stutter before the edges of his vision started to blur and he began to feel warm. "You knew who I was and you didn't tell me?"

"I'm sorry," Liam said. "I wanted to tell you, but I didn't know how."

Edgar snickered and tried to ignore the steadily growing dizziness and warmth threatening to overcome him. "Great. Here I am falling for you and you've been lying to me since we met."

Liam smiled despite Edgar's anger. "You're falling for me?"

"Oh, please," Edgar responded, angry he became vulnerable, even if it was temporary. He wouldn't make the same mistake again. "Well, it's been great, but I'll find a ride back to the motel. I guess I have some research to do about *Dispatching David* and my celebrity life."

"I'll bring you back to the motel," Liam offered. "I don't want you to be alone when you find out."

"When I find out what?" Edgar asked as the handsome, dark-haired man's blood-soaked body flashed through his mind again.

Liam's face softened. "Please let me go with you. I promise it will be better if I'm there. I'll tell you everything I know about you and the show."

"Why didn't you tell me the truth?"

"I thought if you knew who you were, if you remembered you're Edgar Peterson, the star of one of the greatest detective shows in America, then you wouldn't give me the time of day and you definitely wouldn't have agreed to go on a date with me," Liam said, his face crestfallen.

Edgar fidgeted against Liam's car, which he still leaned against. "I guess I understand. But I'm still upset you weren't honest with me this whole time."

"I'm really sorry, Edgar. I'll be completely honest with you from now on."

"Okay, I'll give you another chance," Edgar said slowly, as the lightheaded feeling intensified.

"I promise you won't regret it. I think this is the start of a great relationship and I would hate to end it when we're still getting to know each other."

"Yeah, okay."

Edgar was abruptly hit with a scene of the good-looking, dark-haired man playing basketball, wearing only long athletic shorts and sneakers, dribbling the ball across the court and smiling at him, teasing him when he wasn't quick enough to steal the ball and prevent him from sinking the basketball into the hoop.

Edgar breathed heavily, his chest rising and falling rapidly, his face flushing pink as the image of the shirtless man smiling at him stayed ingrained in his memory. It was him again.

"Do you know who he is?" Edgar suddenly blurted out to Liam. "I mean–" He started to say, remembering he hadn't wanted to tell Liam about his flashbacks, especially because they involved another man, potentially one he had a relationship with.

"Who?" Liam asked, looking bewildered and concerned. "Are you okay, Edgar?"

"I think so, but I keep having flashbacks of a man. At least, I think they're flashbacks or memories, but there's no way to know for sure."

"Who is he?"

"I wish I knew. He's tall with short, dark hair and twinkling green eyes I could get lost staring into. And his smile is like—"

Liam held out his hands to stop Edgar. "Okay, okay. I get it. I don't want to hear any more about this hunk. Let's go back to your motel room and we can try to sort it out. Does that sound okay?"

Edgar exhaled deeply and straightened his posture. "Okay. We can go."

"And maybe you should see a doctor to get checked out—"

"No," Edgar interrupted. "I'm fine."

"Are you sure? I think talking to a doctor could help with your amnesia and your other symptoms."

"What other symptoms?" Edgar asked coldly. I don't need to see a doctor."

Liam and Edgar entered the car, both knowing their relationship would never be the same. They had only known each other for a few weeks, but the foundation of their relationship was built on lies.

# Chapter 6: Delia

Delia was still shaken after her run-in with Blaine, but she was proud of how calm and collected she remained throughout the situation. All her training came back to her and she reacted as she would have if she were still a police officer. It was important to Delia to not forget who she used to be, but she also thought she should be moving on and focusing on the future. She had enough issues to worry about, between her mom's deteriorating mental state and encroaching presence at home, her job where she wasn't reaching her full potential– she couldn't handle much more.

Since Delia's mom was unable to take care of herself, Delia thought it was best to hire a nurse to check on her mom during the day while she was at work, but she still worried something would happen. She kept imagining being at work and receiving a phone call that her mom left the stove on and died in a fire or left the apartment and wandered off. As she pulled into the parking lot at The Fox Luxury Apartments, she paused for a few minutes to collect her thoughts. She didn't want to enter her workspace while she was anxious and worried about things she couldn't control.

When she walked inside, Will greeted her with his usual friendly smile. "Morning, Delia," he said, cheerily.

"Good morning, Will," she answered, setting down her purse and hanging up her coat on the hook. "Any plans for the weekend?"

"Oh, you know me. Hitting up all the bars this weekend," he said dryly.

Will was a widower. His wife died several years ago from breast cancer. He kept to himself since his wife passed away. Besides, he was more the type of person who would be caught at a coffee shop or a museum on the weekend, rather than bar hopping or clubbing.

"Maybe I'll meet you there," Delia joked back. It was a nice change having a boss with whom she felt comfortable around and could joke around with, one who felt more like a friend than a supervisor.

Will shook his head, laughing, and handed Delia the schedule for the upcoming week. "I gave you two days off next week, so I expect you to take them off and not pick up shifts on those days, alright?"

"Alright," Delia agreed, wondering what she could do with her days off. There were a multitude of tasks she *could* be doing, one of those being finding a suitable and affordable assisted living facility for her mom. But the real question was: what did she *want* to be doing? She couldn't shake the encounter with Blaine from her mind and stood lost in thought for several minutes before Will brought her out of it.

"Okay, what's going on?" Will asked. "You seem distracted."

Delia sighed exasperatedly and crossed her arms over her chest. "I don't want to talk about it."

"You sure? In my opinion, talking always helps. Maybe I can bring a fresh perspective to the situation." Will smiled gently, patient as always.

"I don't know. I had a run-in last night with someone from…the last case I worked on–"

Will immediately cut her off. "What? Who was it? Are you okay?"

"I'm fine, but it made me start thinking about the case again. Though, truth be told, I never *stopped* thinking about it. It's been haunting me. I'm not happy with the way it ended. It was never resolved, but the police chief and the other officers were perfectly happy with calling it a murder-suicide and closing the case, even though all the clues pointed to someone else being involved. I'll never understand how you can claim you're working for the law and then let someone get away with a crime, much less multiple murders. I believe in justice. I can't sit by and–"

Will interrupted Delia again. "Delia, I think I know you pretty well after working with you the past few months. I also think reopening the case and hunting down the person responsible for those crimes is what you want to be doing right now. I won't be offended if you quit. I understand you feel it's your responsibility to solve the case once and for all."

Delia uncrossed her arms and paced across the room. "That's just it, Will. I'm not sure if I even want to reopen the case. Do I want to go down that rabbit hole again? It would be more disappointing if I let Edgar escape a second time without being able to prove he committed those crimes."

"You'll figure it out. If it's the right thing to do, God will let you know one way or another."

***

Delia texted Becca and asked if they could meet for coffee at a café near her apartment. Delia ordered a hot chocolate and waited for Becca to arrive. The café served coffee in large, mismatched porcelain mugs. It was a nice touch, not to mention the fact that it was better for the environment. Another positive was that the mugs were nearly the size of soup bowls, the kind you had to hold with two hands. Delia thought Lorelai and Rory from *Gilmore Girls* would approve. The server handed Delia her order of hot chocolate in an enormous white mug with whales on it. Delia contemplated the dessert menu, wondering if she should order a chocolate chip cookie or a double fudge brownie. Becca finally arrived fifteen minutes late.

"Traffic was terrible," Becca exclaimed, throwing down her purse and coat and sitting across from Delia at the table. She adjusted several stray blue hairs that fell from her bun in her haste and waved over the waitress to order a regular coffee with cream and sugar.

Delia laughed and shook her head back and forth. "It's New York City. Traffic is always terrible."

"It was *particularly* terrible today, Delia. So, why did you want to meet up tonight? You usually don't make last-minute plans. Is your mom okay?"

"Yeah, Mom is as fine as she can be. An…incident happened last night, but I don't want you to panic because I'm fine. I need your advice."

"Oh no, what now?" Becca asked, immediately starting to chew on her nails out of habit.

The server came over with Becca's coffee, in a light blue mug with dolphins on it. Perhaps the café was going for an aquatic theme today.

Delia gathered her composure before jumping into the story. She debated if she should even tell Becca, but she was her best friend and she valued her opinion more than anyone. Besides, it wasn't the same as telling Will about the situation. Yes, she liked and respected Will, but he had only known her for a few months. Becca had known her since high school, so she would have more insight about what Delia should do. She could help her decide.

"What do you think?" Delia asked when she finished explaining how Blaine showed up outside her apartment last night and tried to kill her.

Becca surprised Delia by remaining remarkably calm throughout the story and sipping her coffee in silence. "I think you're only asking me because you're scared of making the decision. You're terrified of what will happen if you go after him. Honestly, I'm terrified too. The last thing I want is for him to harm you."

Delia nodded. Becca was right. "I'm sorry, Becca. I shouldn't be putting this decision on you and you're right; I'm terrified. But I'm still not sure if tracking Edgar down will make me feel better."

Delia wondered if she would feel an enormous sense of relief if she could find him, somehow prove he murdered Jackson and Clara, and ensure he rotted in prison for the rest of his pathetic life. She fiddled with her whale coffee mug, staring into the milky brown hot chocolate.

"What's going to happen if you don't do it?" Becca asked wisely, eerily echoing what Delia wondered as well.

Delia groaned. "I know I'll regret it if I don't try, but I can't do it on my own."

Becca's eyes widened as she sipped her coffee. "You aren't asking me to join you, right?"

Delia laughed loudly, nearly spitting out her gulp of hot chocolate. "Absolutely not. I have someone else in mind. Besides, I would never put you in danger."

Becca breathed a sigh of relief. "Thank God. I would much rather write murder mysteries than be in one."

***

Delia came home to find her mom attempting to make dinner. She didn't see the nurse anywhere, so she rushed into the kitchen to confirm there wasn't a fire and her mom wasn't injured.

Her mom scowled as Delia rushed towards her. "Delia, I'm fine!" She exclaimed. "I wanted to make dinner for you. I feel so badly about putting you out. I know you don't want me staying with you forever."

Delia smiled. "It's not a problem, Mom. I want to help you as much as I can. Thanks for making dinner." She paused, eyeing the mess on the stovetop and faux granite countertop. "What are you making?"

Her mom surveyed the pot bubbling on the stove, full of water, and the bags of frozen chicken and veggies still sitting on the counter, and stepped away from the stove, suddenly confused.

"It's okay. Go watch TV. I'll finish cooking." Delia quickly threw the frozen veggies into the boiling water and started thawing the chicken in the microwave.

Her mom wandered into the living room and sat on the couch, staring blankly at the TV. She made a noise of anguish and Delia ran over to see what was wrong.

"Mom? Are you okay?"

Her mom didn't respond and instead pointed at the TV, making the same exaggerated sound of anguish, but not speaking.

"The remote is right here," Delia said, pointing to the ottoman where she always kept the TV remote. "All you have to do is push the red button. See?" Delia pressed the button and the TV powered on.

Her mom snatched the remote from her hands and fiddled with it, turning the volume up and down and flipping through channels. She finally chose a channel and settled into the couch to watch *Goosebumps*.

"We used to watch this when you were little," Delia's mom said suddenly. "Remember? We watched it together." She chuckled to herself. "You were scared of it though."

The apartment was tiny– "open concept" –so Delia could see the TV from the kitchen. Delia chuckled. "I wasn't scared of *Goosebumps*! I loved it."

Delia's mom chuckled again. "No, you used to cower by me when we watched episodes."

"Well, why did you let me watch it, then?" Delia asked incredulously.

"You were scared of everything when you were young. I wanted to toughen you up. I know it worked because you're strong now."

"Thanks, Mom," Delia said with a small smile, going back to the kitchen to finish cooking dinner.

Her mom was right though. Even if she was terrified of whatever monsters were hiding in the darkness, she knew she could face them.

# Chapter 7: Edgar

Liam lounged on the bed in Edgar's motel room, while Edgar sat in one of the uncomfortable wooden chairs. Edgar browsed through the Google search results of "Edgar Peterson." The first article that popped up read "Jackson Birkman, Star of *Dispatching David*, Dies in Tragic Accident." Edgar clicked on the article and quickly skimmed the information, stopping when he saw a photo of Jackson. It was the dark-haired man from his flashbacks. The same man in the photo in his duffel bag. In the photo in the article, Jackson grinned with his arms wrapped around a petite woman with long blonde hair. The photo was captioned "Jackson Birkman with his Fiancée, Clara Rogers." That answered a few of Edgar's questions. He acted with Jackson on the detective show *Dispatching David* and Jackson was engaged to a woman. It seemed likely they were never involved romantically, so why did Edgar have a photo of Jackson in his duffel bag? Clearly, the photo was important enough for him to want it with him when he traveled to Mexico.

As Edgar stared at the photo of Jackson and Clara, he felt his face flush and black spots danced in front of him. As the dizziness overcame him, he found himself standing near the doorway in an apartment. Clara yelled at him to get out. She tried to make him leave, but he forced his way into the apartment and dragged her by her long blonde hair into the bedroom. Edgar slipped on the gloves stashed in his pocket and pulled out a gun. Clara screamed, pleading with him to let her go, kicking and scratching him, trying her best to escape his grip. But she didn't have the physical strength or the knowledge to fight and he ignored her pleas. Edgar threw Clara down on the bed and shot her in the head, blood instantly soaking the silk pillow and her pretty blonde hair. She screamed hoarsely until her last breath faded. He set the suicide note he wrote for her on the nightstand.

With a start, Edgar came back to reality. Was the memory real? Did he kill Clara or was he suffering from a guilty conscience? How could he know the truth? But, the most important question of all: if he committed these terrible acts, did he want to know the truth? Could he live with himself if he had murdered someone? What would Liam think if he knew?

"Are you okay?" Liam asked softly from where he perched on the lumpy motel bed.

Edgar turned to face him. "Honestly, I'm not sure how to feel. Jackson and Clara are dead, but I don't remember them. Is it bad if I don't feel upset? I feel guilty for not remembering, but maybe it's easier this way. It's less painful to forget."

"I'm so sorry, Edgar. Give yourself permission to feel however you need to. It's a strange situation, so I don't blame you for being unsure about your emotions. I can't begin to imagine what you're going through."

"Thanks."

Edgar continued browsing the article, reading about how Jackson starred on the show with his childhood best friend, Edgar Peterson, and how they were inseparable. There was a photo of the two men together on the set of the show. They were in the middle of a heated scene where they were arguing. Edgar stared at the photo, wondering what their friendship was like. The article went on to explain Jackson and Edgar were filming the last scene for the show, when Edgar pulled the trigger on what was supposed to be a prop gun, and killed Jackson almost instantly. The reporter of the article theorized the prop gun must have been switched with a real gun. Someone planted the gun intending for Edgar to murder his best friend.

Edgar felt immense sadness knowing one of his close friends was dead and it was his fault. At least partially. After all, he was the one who pulled the trigger. But he didn't feel the unbearable grief most people would feel after losing a loved one. Despite everything he read about Jackson's life and his own life online, Edgar still didn't have most of his memories back. The worst part was not remembering.

"Do you want to talk about it?" Liam asked, scooting towards the edge of the bed closer to Edgar, but being careful to still give him space.

"According to this article I found online, I'm from Minneapolis, Minnesota," Edgar said, ignoring Liam's question and pointing to the information on his phone so Liam could read it. "I grew up there, so my parents might still live there. I think I should go see them. Maybe they can help me."

"Okay. If that's what you want. But I'm coming with you," Liam said excitedly.

"No. Liam, you've built a life for yourself here. I couldn't ask you to leave all that behind for me." Edgar went back to browsing on his phone without looking up at Liam. "Plus, I'm not exactly happy with you for lying to me. You knew I suffered from memory loss and you recognized me when we met, but you didn't tell me the truth!" Edgar said, his voice becoming louder as his anger returned.

Liam snorted and shook his head. "Edgar, I don't have much of a life here. I work as a bartender at a restaurant, I live in a crappy apartment, I barely have any friends, at least none that would be hard to say goodbye to, and I don't have a family. I'm sorry I lied to you, but I didn't think you would give me a chance if you knew the truth. I know you care about me and I can help you. I'm coming with you."

Edgar stared at Liam, puzzled. He tilted his head to the side and eyed him suspiciously. "Why do you want to help me so badly? We barely know each other."

"I'm aware we've only known each other a few weeks, but I felt a spark when our eyes first met. Didn't you feel it too? I'm sure you did," Liam said earnestly, as he stood from the bed and walked over to Edgar to hold his hands.

Edgar laughed sarcastically. "I don't think my life is going the way I planned, so at this point, I've decided I'm going to take whatever piece of happiness I can obtain. If that means being with you, then that's what I'm going to do."

"I like the way you think. We should embrace the good in our lives. I guess I should go home and pack then," Liam said, smiling broadly. "I'll come by tomorrow and we can head out whenever you're ready. I'll have to talk to Miguel before we go too. I feel a little guilty both of us will be quitting at the same time."

"Sounds like a plan. I'll pack tonight too," Edgar said. He glanced around the motel room that had been his home for over a month. "Not that I have much to pack."

"I'll see you tomorrow, Edgar," Liam said, waving and heading out of the motel room.

"Bye, Liam," Edgar mumbled, as he gathered his belongings.

It wouldn't take Edgar long to pack the few items he compiled since arriving in Mexico. All he needed was the duffel bag with his prized possessions that he had with him when he first woke up near Lake Chapala. After he finished packing, he reflected on the day's whirlwind events. Finding out he was an actor on an award-winning TV show, learning his best friend and fiancée had been killed, realizing he cared about Liam… It was all too much for Edgar.

He left the motel in search of liquor. He vaguely remembered seeing a liquor store nearby, so he ventured into the city by himself for the first time since the day he wandered into Sofia's Cocina and Tequilería. He stumbled across a shady-looking liquor store and went inside, grabbing the first bottle of whiskey he saw on the bottom shelf. Cheap whiskey was fine for a night like this. He wasn't even sure if he liked whiskey, but he would get drunk regardless. He walked back to his motel room to drink the fifth of whiskey by himself.

At first, the whiskey burned and he choked it down. The more he drank, the deeper he scrolled through the trenches of the Internet. What else was he supposed to do after finding out he was a celebrity and connected to not one, but *two murders*? He couldn't find much information about his childhood or his family, other than his earlier discovery that he was raised in Minneapolis and moved to NYC later when Jackson helped him land the role on *Dispatching David*.

When Edgar finished about three-fourths of the bottle of whiskey, he didn't mind the taste anymore and the burning sensation didn't bother him as much. He knew he was too drunk and should probably cut himself off, drink some water, and eat something, so he didn't push his limit. He didn't want to puke or have a hangover tomorrow. But those were problems for future Edgar to worry about. He was past the point of thinking clearly.

Edgar stood up from the bed to use the bathroom, but the room spun around him, the edges of his vision blurring. He tried to grab the chair closest to the bed to stop himself from falling as he lost his balance. Jackson appeared in the room with him, sitting in the other wooden chair. His short, dark hair was matted with dried blood and there was a gaping hole in his head with chunks of rotting flesh crumbling away. His eyes looked hollow and lifeless. Spots appeared around the edges of Edgar's vision as the darkness closed in.

"Did you miss me?" Jackson asked, smiling coyly.

# Chapter 8: Delia

Delia knew she couldn't hunt down Edgar and capture him by herself. She needed backup and she knew the perfect person to call. When she called him, she asked if they could meet at a coffee shop under the pretense of wanting to catch up, but he wasn't dumb and would know Delia was up to something.

Delia was shocked to arrive at the coffee shop and find that her friend had already grabbed a table for them. Her shock most likely came from her years of friendship with Becca and dealing with her perpetual tardiness. She appreciated that a person existed who was even more punctual than her. She approached the table and reached out to shake the hand of the burly, mustached man she was meeting.

"Delia," he said, brushing away her hand and instead engulfing her in a tight hug.

"Oh! Nice to see you again, Jerry," she said.

"Sorry for the unexpected hug," Jerry said, awkwardly grinning.

"It's fine. Just took me off guard. Did you order yet?"

"No, I waited on you. I can grab us some coffee though."

"Oh, no thanks. I don't like coffee."

Jerry raised an eyebrow. "And you wanted to meet at a coffee shop—why exactly?"

"It's usually the best place to discuss business. A neutral, public setting. Plus, meeting at a coffee shop doesn't bring as much pressure as meeting at a restaurant. You don't have to stay for hours. You aren't expected to eat, but still have a drink to take your attention away from the conversation."

"Uh huh. So, what do you want then?"

"A hot tea would be great. Thank you."

Jerry returned several moments later with his steaming mug of coffee and a mug of hot tea for Delia. "A cop who doesn't like coffee," Jerry said, jokingly shaking his head. "You're breaking all the stereotypes, aren't you?"

"Actually, I'm not a police officer anymore. I quit a few months ago. After…you know…"

Jerry smiled sadly. "Yeah, I took some time off after I heard about Jackson and Clara too. It damn near broke my heart when I found out they closed the case because it was deemed a murder-suicide. I still don't know how the investigating officers fucked up so badly. I'm not blaming you for the outcome, of course. I'm sure you did what you could."

Delia blew on her still steaming mug of tea and sipped thoughtfully. She had rehearsed for this conversation, but suddenly felt terrified about what would happen if Jerry declined her proposition. She arrived for the meeting assuming he would say yes, but maybe he wouldn't.

"There's no use in making idle chitchat," Jerry said, interrupting Delia's anxiety-ridden thoughts. "Let's get down to it. Why did you ask to meet with me?"

Delia exhaled slowly, steeling herself for the conversation. "Right. As you said, I tried my best to apprehend the murderer during the Jackson Birkman case—"

"Who was it? Who killed them?" Jerry cut her off, leaning forward conspiratorially.

"Edgar Peterson. Jackson's best friend," she said quietly, mimicking Jerry and leaning across the table so no one else in the crowded coffee shop could hear her.

"Shit! I should have known it was him. It makes sense it was someone close to both of them. He probably had access to Jackson's car. He acted with Jackson on the set of *Dispatching David*, so he easily could have switched the guns. He might have had a key to their apartment too." Jerry stroked his well-groomed mustache thoughtfully, pondering. "Any idea about his motive? What drove him to do that to his best friend?"

Delia pursed her lips. "I've been wondering that too. The biggest problem was the show Edgar put on throughout the investigation. Jackson might have been the star of *Dispatching David*, but Edgar is a talented actor and a convincing liar, especially when his life is at stake."

"I believe it. You would have to be a good liar to evade the terrible things he did. So, did you want to talk it through, try to figure out the weak points in the case that resulted in Edgar being absolved?"

"Not exactly, although we should at some point," Delia said, clearing her throat nervously. "I asked you to meet me here because I was wondering if you want to partner up with me. I'm not sure where Edgar is. He hasn't been on the news and hasn't been seen in months. For all I know, he may have fled the country. First, we have to come up with a plan, then figure out where Edgar is, and track him down."

Jerry nodded. "Then what? Kill him?" He asked with a mischievous grin.

Delia looked appalled. "Of course not. I may be a *former* police officer, but I *do* still have integrity. I intend to reopen the case, while following the law to the best of my abilities. However, the law failed me once before so if we have to…let's say, break the rules a little, I won't be too heartbroken."

"Okay, I understand. I've gotta warn you. This isn't like my typical cases. I mostly handle domestic cases dealing with abuse or child custody. I rarely work on homicide cases, especially not homicides involving celebrities. But this one is personal. I still remember how scared Jackson was the day I found him on the side of the highway after he was kidnapped. He was terrified for his life."

"I remember that day too. I was the first officer Jackson talked to about the kidnapping, then I brought him home and Clara was beside herself," Delia said, chuckling as she remembered how Jackson's tiny fiancée had tried to help him walk inside the apartment building, despite his severe injuries. "I was one of the officers staking out the apartment until the police chief decided it wasn't worth it and we were taken off surveillance. I tried pleading with him, but he didn't think anything was going to happen. I know it isn't common for police officers to have constant surveillance on someone, but it seemed necessary at the time. When I look back on it, I bet Edgar knew. I'm sure of it. He was watching us and keeping an eye on the apartment building, so he knew the second we left." Delia sipped her tea, which was now lukewarm and hurriedly finished it before it became too cold.

The silence stretched between them.

"And of course I'll pay you for your investigative services!" Delia said hurriedly, wondering if that was why Jerry hadn't answered yet. "I'm not sure how much you charge, but—"

"I'll do it," Jerry said, interrupting her. "Don't worry about the money. I liked Jackson and I hate to think about Edgar eluding from his crimes. Jackson and Clara were so young. They were young and engaged, with their whole lives ahead of them. And as far as Edgar goes, who knows what he's been doing since then? Like you said, if he fled the country or at least left New York, he might be hard to find. But murderers never stop for long. If Edgar is the one who did it, then he will kill again and we will find him when he does."

# Chapter 9: Edgar

Edgar and Liam decided to drive to Minneapolis. Since Liam owned a Dodge Challenger and didn't want to leave it in Mexico, it seemed like the best solution. They agreed a road trip together would be fun. It was a good way for them to learn more about each other because it was a thirty-three-hour drive to Edgar's parent's house. Along the way, they could stop for tourist attractions, explore any cities they wanted to see, stay in crappy motels together, and eat junk food anywhere they could find it.

Since Edgar didn't have any form of identification, he contacted the closest U.S. Embassy to report his lost passport and request a new one. After researching the process, Edgar knew it could take several weeks for him to receive his new passport, so they wouldn't be able to leave Mexico immediately. Matters were more complicated because he didn't have proof of his U.S. citizenship, but he hoped he could convince the consular officer to assist him.

Liam drove Edgar to the U.S. Embassy nearby in case he needed an interpreter. Liam was fluent in Spanish after years of living in Mexico and being immersed in the language.

When they arrived at the Embassy, they approached the first available consular officer. She was a heavy-set woman with dark skin, wavy black hair streaked with gray, and a name tag with "Monica" on it. She immediately looked up from her phone with a half-smile and tucked her phone into her desk drawer.

"Hello, I'm Monica. How can I help you?" She greeted them.

"Hi," Edgar said quietly. "I'm visiting Mexico and plan to return home soon, but unfortunately I lost my passport. I would like to apply for a replacement so I can go back to the U.S."

"Okay. Do you have proof of U.S. citizenship, a passport photo, and the required forms filled out?"

Edgar nervously looked at Liam and shook his head.

Liam stepped forward and beamed charmingly at Monica. "So, this is a weird situation, but his name is Edgar Peterson. He was one of the starring actors on the detective show, *Dispatching David*. Maybe you've heard of it?"

Monica stared obviously at Edgar and her mouth dropped open in shock. "Oh my God! I thought you looked familiar, but I wasn't sure why. I *loved* the show!" She said excitedly. "I watched it every week. My husband wasn't really a fan, so I watched it by myself when he worked late. He gets squeamish from gore and violence—"

Edgar cut Monica off and snatched a pen from her desk. "Sorry to interrupt, but how would you feel about an autograph?" He asked, trying his best to mimic Liam's winning smile.

Monica nodded enthusiastically, then stopped and folded her hands on the desk. "Wait a minute. I still need the required forms to file for an emergency passport for you."

Edgar ran his hand through his long hair. "I can fill out the paperwork you need, but is there a way you can look up my previous passport electronically? I don't have another form of ID with me here."

"Hmm, yes, I believe I can. It could take up to 15 days for you to receive your replacement passport," Monica said.

After Monica confirmed she could retrieve Edgar's original passport information and proof of U.S. citizenship electronically, he signed a sparkly notebook she had stashed away in her desk. She beamed when he handed the signed notebook back to her and Edgar smiled back. He didn't remember what it felt like to be a celebrity, but right now, it felt great.

Edgar and Liam left the Embassy and decided to go out for dinner. Edgar wanted to make the most out of his time left in Mexico.

"I know a great burger place we can go to," Liam offered.

"Sure, burgers are fine," Edgar replied.

When they arrived at the restaurant and sat across from each other in a vinyl booth, Edgar browsed the menu while Liam kept glancing surreptitiously at Edgar over the top of his own menu. Finally, Edgar slammed his menu down on the laminate table, which was sticky with remnants of condiments from the previous customers.

"What?" Edgar asked harshly.

Liam set down his menu and tousled his short, black hair. "Nothing."

"Liam, you keep staring at me like I have three heads. What's wrong?"

"It's just—I didn't know how you were going to react after meeting fans of your show. Does it…change anything?" Liam asked, biting his lip and looking at the table.

"What would it change?" Edgar asked, now more confused than irritated. "I still don't have my memory back. You don't know how terrifying it is, not knowing who you are or what you've done. It's like there's this shadow over my mind, clouding my past. Sometimes it feels like the shadow's growing longer," he said quietly, his eyes wide with fear.

"That sounds a bit dramatic."

"Well, I *am* an actor."

"I don't know, Edgar," Liam responded, changing the subject again. "You must have millions stashed away somewhere. Don't you wonder where all your money is?"

Edgar crossed his arms over his thin chest, shaken out of his musings. "Are you after my money?"

"No! That's not what I—it came out wrong. I guess I'm wondering what you did with your money, why you didn't bring it all with you… Why hasn't your family been looking for you? And why did you leave New York?"

Edgar snorted and went back to perusing the menu. "Yeah, I wish I knew too."

# Chapter 10: Delia

After her meeting with Jerry, Delia allowed herself to research Edgar Peterson again. She avoided it for the past few months, but wanted to find out as much as possible before they embarked on their journey. First, she wanted to find out where he might have gone. Was he the type of person who would flee the country to escape because he was scared he could still be convicted? Or did he still live in his swanky Upper East Side apartment without fear of being caught? After perusing her old notes on the case, she refreshed her memory and discovered Edgar was from Minneapolis, Minnesota. She also found out his parents still owned a house in Minneapolis, making it likely they resided there. Edgar's parent's house was a potential safe place for him. She didn't know of any other friends Edgar might have been close to and he didn't have any siblings. She decided she needed to visit the last address listed for Edgar in the city before she could decide what to do next. After all, it would be far easier if they didn't have to leave New York to apprehend him. She would only go to Minneapolis after she exhausted her other options.

Delia tried not to think about how she and Jerry would handle the situation if they needed to travel to Minneapolis. They would have to involve the Minneapolis Police Department, obtain a search warrant for the Peterson's house, and convince a police officer there was reasonable cause to arrest Edgar. Without involving the Minneapolis Police Department, Delia and Jerry would be operating outside the law and Delia would be breaking her own ethics code. Neither of the options were ideal, but Delia knew when the time came, she would do whatever was necessary if it meant Edgar was sent to prison.

Delia drove to Edgar's apartment, hoping he still lived there, while also knowing it was probably futile. Even if he never left the city, he had probably moved. She entered the apartment building and walked up several flights of stairs to the fourth floor. She knocked hard on the apartment door and waited. A young boy wearing Batman pajamas answered the door. He looked like he was five or six.

"Hi," the young boy said.

"Hey," Delia said, kindly. "Are your parents here?"

"Who's there?" A deep voice called from further inside the apartment.

A middle-aged man with curly black hair, wearing sweatpants and a t-shirt came to the door.

"Ollie, I told you not to open the door for strangers," the man said, shaking his head. "Go to your room."

The man turned back to Delia. "Sorry, he loves talking to people. He's too friendly. But we don't want whatever you're selling. And if it's religion you're here to talk about, we're Christian, so we don't want to hear about that either."

"Sorry to stop by like this, but I'm looking for a man named Edgar Peterson. This apartment was his last known address and he's a suspect in a case I'm working on."

The man's eyes widened as he partially closed the apartment door. "I don't know the former renter, so I wouldn't be any help. My son and I moved in a few months ago. Sorry," he said, shutting the door in Delia's face.

Delia sighed. She knew it wouldn't be easy, but still felt defeated as she descended the stairs back to the ground floor and walked to her car parked across the street. Now what? She knew she should go to the NYPD 19th Precinct where she formerly worked and talk to the police chief about reopening the Jackson Birkman case, otherwise she was delving into sketchy territory. On the other hand, if the police chief refused to reopen the case, which he likely would since there wasn't any new evidence to prove Edgar murdered Jackson and Clara, then Delia wouldn't be able to move forward with hunting down Edgar and doing it the right way. Her mind spun as she tried to decide what to do next. Meanwhile, Edgar could be killing someone as she debated her next step.

Delia imagined a pile of dead bodies stacking up, one on top of the other, growing exponentially taller and decaying as she wasted time debating her next move. The mental image made her stomach turn. For the hundredth time, she remembered seeing Clara's body splayed out on the king-sized bed, the silk pillowcase soaked with the blood from the gunshot to her head, her waist-length blonde hair a bloody mess on the pillow.

Delia shook her head as if to rid herself of the memories. Some things were better left forgotten, especially when involving the brutal crime scene of someone she knew. When Delia returned home, her mom was sitting on the couch right where she left her, still mindlessly watching TV.

"Hey, Mom. I'm going on a trip soon," Delia said, sitting beside her mom on the couch.

"Oh. Where are you going?" Her mom asked, not taking her eyes off the TV.

"I have to fly to Minneapolis for a case. There are some loose ends I have to tie up."

"Is it dangerous?" Her mom questioned, turning to face her. "Are you going by yourself?"

"No, I'll be going with an acquaintance. His name is Jerry. He's been a private detective for over 25 years," Delia explained, avoiding telling her mom that, yes, it was a dangerous case.

"Okay. When will you be back?"

"I'm not sure, Mom. I hate doing this, but I don't feel comfortable leaving you alone here. I could be gone for a few weeks, maybe even months, so I'm going to take you to see an assisted living facility today. You can meet the director who runs the memory care unit and tour the place to see if you like it. I already met with them a few weeks ago and put in an application. You've been on a waiting list, but a spot opened up today. The facility is really nice. They have weekend movie nights and there's a shuttle you can take to the grocery store and a few other places in town. You will only be able to leave under supervision or if I visit and take you somewhere. But you'll be safe and that's the important thing. They will take good care of you and I'll come visit you as much as I can."

Her mom stared at her, unblinking and unmoving.

"Mom? Did you hear me?"

"No!" Her mom whispered piercingly. "No, no, no!" She said loudly, jumping up from the couch and throwing the TV remote across the room. "I'm not going. You can't lock me away and eradicate me."

"I'm sorry," Delia said, taking a few steps back, her eyes beginning to blur with tears. "I don't have a choice. There's no one else who can make sure you don't harm yourself while I'm gone. I can't take care of you and you can't live by yourself anymore."

"I'm fine! I'm not crazy. I've been living on my own for over twenty years and I will live alone until I die," her mom said fiercely.

"You can't be alone. I don't want something to happen to you," Delia said, her chest heaving as she fought back tears. This was turning out to be harder than she expected.

"I'm not going. You can't make me. I'm your mom and you're my daughter, not the other way around," Delia's mom spat. Her chest rose and fell rapidly and she clenched her fists as she tried to control her agitation.

"I know, but this is the best option for both of us. Will you please tour the assisted living facility with me and give it a chance? If you hate it, then I promise we can find a different place together."

Her mom stalled for a moment, slowing her thinking. "Fine, I'll tour it, but I'm not going to like it."

"Please go in with an open mind," Delia begged. "I think you'll be surprised when you have a chance to look around and meet some of the employees. Besides, I'm not going to force you to live there if you feel so strongly about it."

"Okay, we can go," her mom said, her breathing finally steadying and returning to normal.

"Grab your coat," said Delia, collecting herself. "Our appointment is in a half hour."

When they arrived at the assisted living facility, her mom didn't say much throughout the tour. She was well-behaved and remained calm. She met the director and a few of the residents in the memory care wing. Delia didn't want to jinx it, hoping her mom was coming around to the idea. She knew it was horrible, but plenty of people made the same decision as her. Not everyone was equipped to handle taking care of an aging parent, especially when they were becoming violent and their mind was rapidly deteriorating. Delia couldn't quit her job to be a full-time caretaker because she needed the money.

Delia and her mom returned to the apartment where her mom finally broke her silence.

"It's fine," she managed to say, deflated. "I'll live there if that's what you want. I understand you don't want me around anymore."

Her mom was resigned to her fate. Her moments of clarity were sometimes the most difficult. At least when she was in one of her fits or confused about what was going on, Delia could blame the Alzheimer's and remind herself it wasn't her mom. She could remember how she acted when her mind was still fully intact and how much she loved her. But moments like these were hard because Delia knew it more closely resembled their reality. Regardless of what either of them wanted, it was the best decision for her mom to live the remainder of her days where she could receive the help she needed.

However, Delia still needed to resolve the issue of being able to afford the astronomical monthly expense. She only had enough money in her savings to safely afford the first few months without tapping into her emergency money or retirement fund, but that was a problem for another day.

***

Delia planned to drop her mom off at the facility tomorrow, then she and Jerry were flying to Minneapolis at the end of the week. Delia had never traveled to Minnesota and wished she were going under different circumstances because Minneapolis intrigued her. She had lived in New York her entire life and barely traveled since work always consumed her adult life.

Delia hoped they would have time to drive by Paisley Park and see Prince's studio and home from the outside or maybe they would be extraordinarily lucky and catch a glimpse of him in downtown Minneapolis. He was known for throwing spontaneous parties at Paisley Park and was constantly spotted at First Avenue. But she knew the focus of their trip was to find Edgar.

Delia and Jerry decided not to talk to the police chief or try to have the case reopened. They didn't have any new evidence that supported Edgar being the murderer. There also wasn't a way to obtain new evidence unless she could access one of the crime scenes, but they were all cleaned months ago. Besides, there was a new family living in Edgar's apartment and there were probably new tenants in Jackson and Clara's apartment as well, which meant she couldn't take another look at the crime scenes or try to obtain Edgar's DNA. Delia knew the risk of her and Jerry going out on their own to track down a murderer, but Delia also knew she wouldn't be able to move on if she didn't try.

Delia gathered the items she thought would be necessary for the trip: her gun and bullets, several outfits, a book to read, wireless earbuds, and several other tools she could need. She also stored digital files on her phone, with notes from when she worked on the Birkman case previously. She planned on reviewing them one more time to see if she could piece it together. Sometimes all it took was one more look at the details for a piece of the puzzle to suddenly fit.

She planned on discussing their plan of attack with Jerry before they tried approaching Edgar. Maybe he wasn't even in Minneapolis. It was their best guess at this point, but he could be anywhere. Delia hoped Edgar's parents would have some information to help them, but she wondered if they would try to protect him if they suspected he was involved in Jackson's death. Since Delia wasn't a parent, it was hard for her to imagine going to such lengths to protect someone if they murdered multiple people, but maybe they would justify it to make themselves feel better. They could convince themselves Edgar had a legitimate reason for killing them. Delia was getting ahead of herself though. For all she knew, Edgar's parents could have moved or they might not be mentally competent. They might not be of any help. It was difficult to think about, but Delia tried her best to prepare herself for any outcome. She knew that in some situations, no matter how much you planned, things didn't turn out the way you expected.

Delia went into the guest bedroom in her apartment, wanting to make sure her mom's belongings were packed and hoped she would be ready to leave soon. However, her mom's clothes were all over the floor and in the laundry hamper, her jewelry was sitting on the nightstand by the bed, and her record collection was scattered throughout the room, which couldn't be good for preserving them.

"Mom, have you started packing?" Delia asked.

"Of course I have," her mom said, pointing to her large, black suitcase on the bed with a few sweaters neatly folded inside it.

"Let me help you." Delia started picking up clothes and folding them, arranging them to maximize space in the suitcase.

"No! You're doing it all wrong!" Her mom screamed, yanking the neatly folded clothes out of the suitcase and throwing them back on the floor.

"Mom, please work with me. I know this is difficult, but I'm trying my best to help you. If there was another option, I would consider it."

"You're trying to get rid of me," her mom said. "You don't want me around anymore so you're sending me to die in that horrible place."

"It's not a horrible place. The director and all the doctors are friendly. I'm sure some of the residents are nice too. Maybe you'll make some friends and have people to spend time with."

"You would like that, wouldn't you? Then you wouldn't have to come visit me," her mom fired back.

"I promise I'm going to visit you as much as possible, but it will probably be a few weeks because I'll be in Minneapolis for a case, remember?" Delia asked, sitting on the queen-sized bed and looking around the messy room in anguish.

"Oh, *that's right*," her mom said sarcastically, as if she could have forgotten. "You're abandoning me. For all I know, you're never coming back."

At this point of the argument, Delia's dog, Lily, became agitated from the situation. She paced the room whining, sensing the tension between the two women.

Delia ignored Lily's whining and started grabbing clothes and throwing them in the suitcase, then picked up a handful of jewelry and was about to toss it in the suitcase when her mom grabbed her wrist to stop her.

"Don't you dare throw my expensive jewelry in there like it's cheap costume jewelry. Most of those rings and earrings were gifts from your father, God rest his soul."

Delia set down the jewelry and began looking for a small Ziploc bag or a container the jewelry could be securely stored in as she continued talking to her mom.

"I'm sorry. I know they're important to you. I'm not abandoning you though. This is hard for me too. I never thought about what I would do if you were sick or couldn't take care of yourself. I didn't want to think about it, but now it's happening and I'm trying my best, but I'm sorry if I'm not handling this right."

Delia's mom found an empty cosmetic case and slipped the jewelry inside. After she set it in the inner pocket of the suitcase, she hugged Delia. "I know. This is hard for both of us. If your father was here…well, then he could take care of me."

"Yeah, but he's not here. The only person you have is me, so you're going to have to deal with it."

Delia and her mom continued packing the room in silence. Delia knew it was probably difficult for her mom to pack up an entire life's worth of belongings and cherished memories. Whether she lived a few more months or years, the outcome would be the same. Death was inevitable and Delia could only imagine how terrifying it must be knowing the end of your existence was near.

Delia still had a few more days until her flight to Minneapolis with Jerry. They agreed it was best if they took time to prepare and try to gather as much information as possible, so they weren't going into the situation blind. She wanted her mom settled in the assisted living facility before she left in case there were any incidents the first few days she was there. Delia was listed as the emergency contact, of course, but if she was out of town and something happened, Becca was the secondary contact. There was no one else Delia could list on the form. Delia pondered the situation, wondering if Becca would be her only emergency contact when she was old and death was inching closer. She wondered if her mom was scared of dying alone, without a single soul by her side.

Delia helped her mom settle in the assisted living facility later in the day with only minor complaining throughout the process. She told her mom to call or text her if she wanted to talk or needed anything. She didn't want her to feel alone. Delia knew that choosing to move her mom to an assisted living home irrevocably changed their relationship, but what choice did she have?

When Delia returned to her apartment, Lily greeted her at the door. One perk when her mom lived with her was that Delia didn't feel as guilty leaving for work because Lily wasn't alone all day. Becca had agreed to watch Lily while she was in Minneapolis and was supposed to stop by to pick her up before Delia's flight at the end of the week.

Delia cooked pasta for dinner because she didn't feel mentally capable of cooking a meal involving more than a handful of ingredients. She sat on the couch in her living room and powered on the TV, flipping through the channels to try to find a show to watch while she ate dinner. She knew it was a bad habit, but it was one she couldn't break. Maybe she constantly needed noise in the background, so she wasn't left alone with her thoughts. The silence was deafening. Or maybe it was Lily's obnoxious snores as she laid stretched out next to Delia on the couch.

As Delia switched the TV from channel to channel, she nearly dropped her bowl of pasta when she saw a man with shaggy, brown hair down to his shoulders and hauntingly dark eyes appear on her flat-screen TV. Lily awoke immediately, eyeing the bowl of pasta.

"What the hell?" Delia mumbled to herself, setting down the remote and placing her pasta bowl on the kitchen counter, so it was out of Lily's reach and leaning closer to the TV.

It was Edgar. The image she saw flash across the TV was a photo taken by an American tourist in Mexico. They spotted him at a fancy rooftop bar near Lake Chapala and snapped the photo on their phone. The TV reporter explained how no one had seen or heard from Edgar in months. Fans and reporters had speculated about what happened to him. Some people thought he would retire from acting so he could live a quiet life away from the press. Others thought he took a break to heal and recover from his grief and the loss of Jackson.

As Delia contemplated how she and Jerry should change their plans, her cellphone rang. Jerry was calling her.

"Hello?" Delia said, swiping up on the phone to answer the call.

"Hey, Delia. I don't know if you saw yet, but apparently Edgar was spotted in Mexico a few days ago."

"Yeah, I was watching E! and saw the photo. I guess we know where he is now," Delia said, slumping down on the couch and wondering if it was too late to cancel their plane tickets and ask for a refund.

"Actually, I don't think he will stay in Mexico for long if he hasn't left already. I bet having tourists recognize him freaked him out. He probably packed up and left quickly after the scene at the bar. I don't know how much of the broadcast you caught, but at the beginning, the reporter said the tourist tried approaching Edgar for an autograph, but he was with a mystery man who kept the tourists away and made them back off," Jerry explained.

"No, I missed the beginning of the story. Wow. What do you think we should do now?"

"I think we should still wait until Friday and fly to Minneapolis as we planned. I bet Edgar is pretty spooked and that's an even better reason for him to want to go somewhere he feels safe, which I'm assuming would be his parent's house."

"I think you're right. It makes sense for him to go there next," Delia paused, processing the newfound information. "Did the reporter say who the mystery man was?"

"Nope, but he's probably someone Edgar met in Mexico. I wouldn't worry about him. Edgar is the target."

"Right."

"Well, I just called to let you know Edgar was spotted. At least we know he's still alive," Jerry said, laughing.

"Thanks for the call. I have a few things I wanted to do tonight, but should we talk more tomorrow?" Delia asked.

"Sure. I'll call you in the afternoon. Talk to you then."

"Bye," Delia said, hanging up her phone.

Delia stared in amazement at Edgar's photo still flashing across the TV with a caption scrolling across the bottom saying, "Edgar Peterson Spotted in Mexico at a Bar with Mystery Man." Delia wondered who the man was with Edgar. She knew she should listen to Jerry and let it go because he probably wasn't important. He could have been a random person at the bar or maybe he was an employee there. Just because he had been standing next to Edgar and tried fending off the tourists didn't necessarily mean they knew each other before the night at the bar or that he was involved with whatever Edgar had been up to. Jerry was right. He was a random person. As far as they knew, Edgar always worked alone. But Delia couldn't stop herself from wondering, what if he wasn't working alone this time? What if he decided he wanted a partner? What then?

# Chapter 11: Edgar

Edgar and Liam spent the next two weeks working at Sofia's, saving their money. Miguel was relieved to have more time to find new waiters and gladly agreed to let them work until they were able to leave Mexico. In their free time, Liam continued showing Edgar around the city. They spent their days wandering the city, having picnics, swimming, and hiking the many mountains near the lake.

When Edgar finally received his new passport, he and Liam decided to have one last picnic at Lake Chapala before they departed on their trip. It was a particularly warm day, so the sun beat down harshly as they walked to the beach. Palm trees lined the beach, the large, green fronds swaying gently in the slight breeze. Kids ran around the lake, splashing each other and screaming, while their parents idly stood by sipping beer. Tourists were rampant in the spring, so they weren't the only Americans at the lake.

Liam spread out a large, plaid blanket on the sand, while Edgar opened the cooler to pull out a hard cider for himself and a beer for Liam. He opened the cans and handed the beer to Liam.

Edgar raised his cider can and touched it to Liam's beer can. "Cheers," he said with a grin. "To life, love, and figuring out the fucking meaning of it all."

Liam chuckled. "I'll toast to that," he said, tapping his can against Edgar's and taking a sip of his beer.

Edgar leaned back on the blanket, resting on his arms and staring at Liam. "Liam, what do you want out of life?" He asked, suddenly.

Liam took a large gulp of his beer and wiped his mouth with his hand. "Hmm. Since moving here, I live day-to-day. I don't plan for the future or worry about what I'll be doing years from now. I guess I want what most people want. To be happy."

Edgar paused, taking a delicate sip of his cider and looking away from Liam's stare. "Yeah, that would be nice," he said softly, wondering what would make him happy. He felt content for the moment, but didn't know how long it would last before his peace was shattered again.

Liam leaned back on the blanket and scooted closer to Edgar, grabbing his hand. "I'm glad we met."

Edgar squeezed Liam's hand and chugged most of the cider. He began to feel dizzy, whether it was from the cider, the sun, or something else entirely, that remained to be seen. His hand became clammy and sweaty in Liam's hand, so he hastily pulled away, blinking rapidly as black spots danced in front of him.

"Edgar? Are you okay?" Liam asked with concern.

"I'm…fine," Edgar responded as Jackson appeared in front of him.

Jackson smirked at him, shaking his blood-soaked head and rolling his eyes. "You were hoping I was going to show up, weren't you?"

"Why would I want you to keep haunting me?" Edgar asked, glaring at Jackson's ghostly form.

"You were in love with me. You want me to be jealous," Jackson said, brushing his fingers through his dark hair, making bits of decomposing flesh crumble away, falling into the formerly pristine sand.

Edgar ignored Jackson's statement. His stomach turned queasy. "If I'm going to see you and be haunted by you, could you at least appear normal and not all decaying and disgusting?"

Liam looked quizzically at Edgar, then at the place where Edgar intently stared. "Uh, what are you talking about?"

"It's nothing," Edgar said quickly, as he unconvincingly tried to reassure Liam of his sanity. He wondered what Liam saw in him. It didn't make sense. What did Liam want? Was he after his money? Did he want to be with him for his fame?

Jackson snorted. "Good job, Edgar. You're going to drive away the only person who cares about you. Stop acting crazy."

Edgar stood from his lounging position on the blanket and immediately became disoriented. Now instead of one corporeal Jackson, he saw two. He scooped up a handful of sand and clumsily threw it in Jackson's direction. "Leave me alone!" He screamed.

Jackson nodded curtly. "Fine, but I know you don't really want me to leave. Don't do anything you're going to regret, Edgar," he said as he vanished.

Edgar looked around in a crazed state of mind, realizing Jackson disappeared. A few people nearby stared with varying looks of worry and confusion. Edgar ignored them and slumped back onto the blanket next to Liam.

"What's going on, Edgar?" Liam asked, eyes wide with apprehension.

"I promise it's nothing," Edgar said, resting his head on Liam's broad shoulder. "I'll take care of it."

"Maybe I should take you back to your hotel room. Sometimes being in the sun for too long can mess with your head."

"Yeah, you're probably right. We should try to sleep, so we're rested for tomorrow. Are you ready for the trip?"

"I can't wait. It's going to be an adventure!" Liam said, his tone suddenly becoming overly enthusiastic.

Liam dropped Edgar off at The Sunset Motel and left shortly after to finish packing. Edgar didn't need much time to pack, but wanted to spend his last night in Mexico by himself. As Edgar lay in bed that night, he pondered again why Liam wanted to be with him. Sure, Liam was a nice guy, but he was kind of creepy. Edgar decided it didn't matter. Liam helped him when he didn't know anyone in Mexico and Liam was his way of returning to the U.S., to find his parents and learn about his past. Once he arrived in Minneapolis, he wouldn't need Liam anymore.

Edgar struggled to fall asleep, imagining Jackson in his motel room with him, sitting in one of the wooden chairs and staring at him through the darkness, his lifeless eyes watching him. He knew Jackson was dead. He was murdered. The Jackson he saw wasn't the *real* Jackson; rather, it was a figment of his overactive imagination. Wasn't it?

# Chapter 12: Delia

The next morning, Delia woke to a quiet apartment, remembering her mom was safely in the assisted living facility. Delia was back to cooking breakfast for one. As she fried eggs in a skillet and heated water for tea on the stove, she thought about what she and Jerry were about to do, the danger of their mission and the risk. Delia felt passionate for the first time in months. She was excited about the case and the prospect of capturing Edgar. She needed to tell Will what was going on. Although he was a great boss and wanted the best for her, Delia still wanted to explain herself. When she talked to him a few days ago, he seemed understanding, but she needed to officially quit her job. It had been a good enough job for a few months. Delia took a massive pay cut and worked long hours, but mostly because she picked up any extra shifts she could.

When she arrived at work, Will was already in the office, pouring coffee in the break room. The smell of freshly brewed coffee permeated the air. Although Delia wasn't a fan of coffee, she didn't find the smell unpleasant.

"Hey, Delia," Will greeted her as she set down her coat and bag.

Delia smiled brightly, despite the knot in her stomach. "Hi, Will."

"Ready to tackle another day?" Will asked, putting the coffeepot back on the warmer and carrying his steaming mug over to his desk.

"I suppose," Delia said, sitting down at her own desk and taking a sip of her Yeti thermos filled with hot tea.

"There's no day like today!" Will said exuberantly, his overwhelmingly positive nature spreading to Delia as usual.

"Actually, I wanted to talk to you…" Delia started.

"Uh oh. Did something else happen? Do you need me to stake out your apartment and take down the man who keeps bothering you?" Will said, smiling.

"No, he hasn't come back. Besides, I can handle it on my own."

"I know you can, Delia. I was teasing you. You're one of the most capable, self-assured people I've ever known."

"Will, I've enjoyed working with you the last few months and I'm grateful you were willing to hire me after I quit the force. I appreciate that you took a chance on me. But I think it's time for me to move on to the next step in my career. I'm sorry to do this on such short notice, but today will be my last day," Delia said quickly, before she could lose her courage.

"I can't say I'm surprised. I always knew you were meant for bigger and better things, although I'm sad to see you go. I'll miss having you around here. Does this have something to do with the case you can't let go of?"

"Yes, but I don't want to give you all the details. It's best if no one else is involved."

"Alright, I understand. Well, I know you'll be careful, but I'm going to tell you anyways. You still have your whole life ahead of you and I would hate for you to miss out on everything life has to offer," Will said, taking a big gulp of his black coffee.

"Thanks, you know I will be," Delia sipped her tea thoughtfully, contemplating Will's comment about missing out on life.

Was she already missing out? Her last serious relationship was years ago. Other than a random date with an old coworker, she couldn't remember her last date. She didn't have any kids. If her mom passed away, she wouldn't have any close family left. Her only close friends were Becca and Joel. She didn't know what to do about her career. In fact, taking a job as a security guard and then quitting after several months proved she didn't know what would be fulfilling. Did a job exist that she could spend the next thirty years working until she could retire? Or was she doomed to forever be stuck in a loop of indecision or making one bad choice after another with her career and relationships until she died old and alone and miserable?

Delia sobbed out loud and covered her mouth in surprise. She didn't want to make a fool of herself at work. She prided herself on staying in control, even when she felt emotional.

"Delia? Are you okay?" Will asked, setting down his coffee and turning from his position at his desk to look directly at her.

"Yes, I'm fine," Delia briskly replied. "I have to use the restroom. I'll be back in a few minutes."

Delia grabbed her purse from the hook near the door and sprinted to the women's bathroom. Once she was inside, she took out her phone and saw several dozen missed text messages, a few phone calls, and a voicemail. She listened to the voicemail first.

"Hi, Delia. This is Jim with Oak Tree Assisted Living. We've tried calling several times but have been unable to reach you. Your mom had a stroke early this morning and she's in the hospital. The name of the hospital is—"

Delia barely listened to the rest of the voicemail before throwing her phone in her purse and running back into the main office.

"Will, my mom had a stroke. The director of the assisted living facility called, but I must have missed his calls. I have to go to the hospital. I don't know how bad it is, but I need to leave right now. I'm sorry."

"Oh, Delia. I'm so sorry about your mom. Of course, leave right away. I'll be praying for her," Will said kindly, patting Delia on the shoulder.

"Thanks for understanding. I'll come by before I leave for Minneapolis to say goodbye to you."

"You're still going to Minneapolis?" Will asked, his eyes widening.

"Of course," Delia responded immediately. No matter what happened, she needed to stop Edgar.

"Well, alright. Good luck."

"Bye, Will," Delia said, running out the door, only stopping to grab her coat.

As she drove to the hospital, she turned on the stereo to listen to the Blue October CD currently in her car. As always, the music soothed her. She couldn't bear to be alone with her thoughts. She needed to make it to the hospital. Delia zoned out while driving, which probably wasn't the best time to do so, but she found herself focusing on the lyrics and not thinking clearly.

When she arrived at the hospital, she parked crookedly in the first available parking spot and barely remembered to lock her car. Delia ran into the hospital, realizing she didn't know which room her mom was in or which floor was for stroke patients. She should have paid more attention to the voicemail.

Delia approached the front desk; wispy strands of her red hair were flying around her flushed face and she forgot to put her coat on despite the cold.

"Hi, my name is Delia Wilson. I'm here to see my mom. She had a stroke," Delia managed to choke out despite the lump in her throat. She brushed several stray hairs behind her ear and attempted to straighten her disheveled appearance.

The woman at the front desk was burly, with short blonde hair cropped below her ears and a kind smile.

"Don't worry, dear. It will be okay," she said. "What's your mom's name? And do you have a photo ID?"

"Yes," Delia said, pulling her driver's license out of her wallet and sliding it across the desk. "Her name is Natalia Wilson."

The woman picked up Delia's driver's license and peered closely at the name and photo before setting it back down. "Okay, she's in Room 305. It's on the third floor. You can take the elevator down the hall to the left," the woman explained, pointing to the elevator around the corner.

"Thank you," Delia said, picking up her driver's license, hoisting her purse higher on her shoulder, and walking towards the elevator.

As Delia entered the elevator and pushed the button for the third floor, she impatiently tapped her foot against the floor, wishing the elevator would go faster. She didn't have time to waste. She wanted to see her mom.

Delia finally slowed down after exiting the elevator. She took several deep breaths, centering herself and preparing for the worst. She didn't know how bad the stroke was and if it would be debilitating. Maybe this was the end. She didn't want to consider the possibility, but her mom might not survive. She was already well into her sixties and although she never dealt with many health issues until recently, the onset of Alzheimer's had already aged her.

Delia knocked on the door of her mom's hospital room, clenching her teeth together. She waited a moment for an answer and when there was none, she gingerly opened the door.

"Hello? Mom?"

Delia entered the room. There were two hospital beds, one of which was empty. In the other bed, there was a woman with long, light brown hair graying at the roots. She wore a hospital gown. Her eyes were closed and she appeared to be asleep as her chest rose and fell gently. An IV in her arm pumped fluids through her body. Delia barely recognized her mom. She looked so fragile. She pulled over one of the chairs near the window and carried it closer to the bed, so she could sit near her mom.

"Mom?" Delia said softly.

There was no answer. Delia assumed her mom was asleep. Well, that was fine. She would stay with her until she woke up. She didn't want her mom to be alone in the hospital. Guilt coursed through her for forcing her mom to stay in the assisted living facility, for not being there when her mom had the stroke, not being the one to call an ambulance or be with her, for not answering the phone when the director initially called her hours ago. There wasn't any point in Delia bearing the weight of guilt now. She reminded herself she was with her mom now and that was what mattered, but it was difficult to shake the crushing weight that she had failed as a daughter when she was the only person looking out for her mom.

Delia whimpered as she dwelled on her mistakes and didn't notice her mom's eyes flickering open.

"Delia? Is that you?" Her mom asked, blinking several times and trying to see more clearly, even though she wasn't wearing her glasses. Her speech sounded slurred, a result of the stroke.

"Yes, Mom, it's me. I'm here," Delia responded, grabbing her mom's hand instinctively and holding it in her own hand.

"I'm glad…you came," her mom said, struggling to form the words and fidgeting in the bed.

"Are you comfortable? Do you need another pillow or a different blanket?"

"More blankets would be nice," her mom said, shivering and trying to pull the thin, fleece blanket up to her chin.

"I'll find a nurse and ask for some. If I thought more before coming here, I would have brought you a change of clothes and some of your belongings and maybe a book or two to read while you're staying here."

"It's fine, Delia."

"No, it's not. I'm sorry I wasn't there for you. I should have been with you. I've been letting this case consume me and…you're more important," Delia said, as a few tears slipped down her cheeks.

"Well, while you're feeling guilty, maybe you could bring me some food too?"

Delia laughed despite her tears. "Sure. I'll be right back."

Delia patted her mom's hand and grabbed her purse, heading towards the cafeteria to buy a meal for her mom. As she walked to the cafeteria, a few more tears slid down her cheeks and she hastily brushed them away. She was trying her best to be strong, but she was on her own. She thought about calling Becca and decided against it; she didn't want Becca and Joel to worry about her more than they already did. Besides, she was tough. She always handled life's challenges by herself and that was exactly what she intended to continue doing.

# Chapter 13: Edgar

The next morning, Liam picked up Edgar at 6:00 a.m. Liam was wide awake and ready to tackle the trip, but Edgar could barely function in the morning.

For the first part of the trip, a silence stretched between them as they both became lost in their own thoughts. They stopped once for gas, grabbed a snack, and stretched their legs, then continued the road trip.

Liam drove once again, while Edgar dozed for several hours, dreaming of Jackson. When Edgar woke up, the sky was dark. He was disoriented and it took him a few minutes to remember where he was and who he was with. He adjusted his pillow and sat up straight in the passenger seat, rubbing his eyes wearily.

"Where are we?" He sleepily asked Liam.

Liam glanced at a sign on the side of the road. "Just passing through San Antonio, Texas."

"When do you want me to drive?"

"I think we can start looking for motel signs and find somewhere to sleep for the night. It's a long trip, so we need to get some rest," Liam reasoned.

Edgar agreed and pointed out a motel after several miles of searching for one. They checked in at the front desk and grabbed their belongings from the car.

The motel was in much worse condition than The Sunset Motel Edgar occupied while living in Lake Chapala. The comforter on the bed looked stained, the bathroom was covered in a layer of grime, and the old-fashioned, box-shaped TV was mounted precariously on the wall across from the bed, looking as if it could fall at any moment. The generic artwork on the walls was bland and uninspiring. There wasn't a mini fridge, microwave, or coffeemaker. The only furniture in the room was a king-sized bed with a nightstand on either side of the bed. Edgar reluctantly concluded he would have to share the bed with Liam.

Liam brushed his teeth in the bathroom while Edgar stood near the bed, thinking about how disgusting the motel was and what types of germs or diseases he could obtain from sleeping in the bed.

Liam came out of the bathroom wearing gray cotton sweatpants and no shirt. "Well, ready for bed?" He asked Edgar, smiling and patting the stained comforter on the bed. "We might not want to sleep with this though," he said, hurriedly removing the comforter and sliding underneath the lighter fleece blanket on top of the sheets.

After Edgar brushed his teeth, removed his contacts, used the bathroom, re-organized his duffel bag, and completed every possible task he could to stall for time, he climbed into bed with Liam.

"Don't worry," Liam said, putting his arm around Edgar when they were finally lying next to each other. "There's no pressure. Goodnight, Edgar."

"Goodnight, Liam," Edgar sighed in relief.

***

Edgar woke up to granola bars, Pop-Tarts, and two steaming cups of coffee sitting on the nightstand.

"Morning," Liam greeted him, coming out of the bathroom with his short, spiky hair wet and wearing a new outfit. "I went to the gas station down the road while you were still sleeping. I couldn't stay in bed any longer."

"Thanks," Edgar said wearily, trying to force himself out of bed. He grabbed one of the coffee cups and took a careful sip. "Ahh."

"Oh shit. Is the coffee terrible? I didn't try it before I brought it back here." Liam took a small sip of the other coffee cup. "Okay, I'm confused. It tastes fine."

"It's too bitter," Edgar said, wrinkling his nose. "I always drink it with cream and sugar."

Liam chuckled. "Sorry. I'll make a mental note for next time."

"It's fine. I'll still drink it."

"As soon as we finish our coffee and eat breakfast, we should hit the road. We have a long drive ahead of us," Liam said.

"Right." Edgar grabbed a blueberry Pop-Tart, ripped off the wrapper, and took a huge bite.

"Well, I'm glad you don't have anything against Pop-Tarts. I'll have to cook for you someday. I know my way around a kitchen."

Edgar laughed. "Good because I don't know how to cook."

A scene jumped into Edgar's mind of opening cupboards and rummaging through soft close drawers in a kitchen with stainless steel appliances and spotless, dark granite countertops. He turned to Jackson, "Okay, you win. Eggs and toast it is."

Jackson snickered and Edgar smiled at him, feeling a wave of happiness rush through him. The room spun and seemed to tilt sideways. Suddenly, he knelt in the kitchen on the cold ceramic floor with Jackson's lifeless body in his arms. There was a gunshot wound in Jackson's head. Blood poured freely from the wound onto Edgar's shirt. He helplessly tried to stop the bleeding, but it was too late. As his hands became soaked in Jackson's blood, he screamed.

"Edgar!" Liam yelled, rushing over and shaking him. "Snap out of it! What's going on?"

Edgar looked down at his hands and turned them over to inspect his palms. They were clean. No blood.

"His blood was on my hands. He was bleeding all over me. I couldn't help him. It's all my fault," Edgar said, slumping onto the bed and hugging one of the pillows.

"Are you talking about Jackson? Because his death was a terrible accident. It wasn't your fault," Liam responded, sitting gingerly next to Edgar on the bed.

"I'm the one who pulled the trigger on the gun," Edgar said. "I'm guilty even if I don't remember what happened."

"Do you remember when he died? Are your memories coming back?" Liam asked.

"Only small scenes. Mostly involving Jackson."

Liam wavered before asking, "Were you in love with him?"

Edgar thought about how he felt during the flashbacks and about the photo of Jackson tucked carefully away in his duffel bag. "No," he said after a long silence.

"That was convincing," Liam said, snorting nervously.

"I'm sorry, Liam. Even if I did love him, I'm not the same person I was then."

"You're right, but it's probably because you've lost most of your memories."

"I don't want to dwell on the past. For now, I want to focus on going to Minneapolis and seeing my parents. I think talking to them will help clear up my past."

"Okay," Liam said, standing and gathering his belongings. "I'm going to start loading our stuff into the car. Be ready in ten minutes." He quickly grabbed as much as he could carry in one trip and left the motel room.

Edgar finished his Pop-Tart and bitter coffee, contemplating Liam's reaction. At first, he seemed worried about Edgar, but then it seemed as if he was only preoccupied with how Edgar felt about Jackson. The truth was it didn't matter how Edgar felt about Jackson, whether he loved him when he was alive or was still in love with him, because he was dead. His best friend was dead and not a single force on Earth could change the past.

"Edgar, are you ready to go?" Liam called from the doorway.

"Yup, be there in a second," he yelled back, shoving the rest of his belongings into his duffel bag and double checking the bathroom to make sure he didn't leave any items behind. He threw the Pop-Tart wrapper and coffee cup in the tiny trash can near the TV and grabbed the remainder of the snacks for the trip.

Once they were in the car again, they sat in silence while Liam drove. Liam suggested he continue driving since Edgar didn't have a driver's license and wasn't sure he remembered all the necessary traffic laws. Liam turned on the radio and fiddled with the knob, changing radio stations until he found classic rock.

"Are you okay with classic rock?" He asked Edgar.

"I think so."

"When do you want to stop again?"

"Whenever you want," Edgar replied. "You're the one driving, so we can stop when you're tired."

The classical rock music wafted from the radio speakers and through the car, the only noise for nearly twenty minutes until Liam broke the silence.

"We're on a road trip. We should do something fun."

"Like what?" Edgar asked.

"I don't know. Something crazy like going skinny dipping in a lake at midnight or stopping at a weird roadside attraction or going outdoor rock climbing."

"We can stop at a roadside attraction if you want, but the other stuff sounds terrifying."

Liam laughed, the sound booming through the enclosed space. "I was kidding. Well, sort of." He drummed his fingers on the steering wheel to the beat of the music. "I wish you knew what your parents are like, so you could prep me before I meet them."

"Huh. I didn't think about it before," Edgar said slowly. "You'll be meeting my parents and I don't know them. This should be fun," he said sarcastically.

"If they're anything like you, then I'm sure it will be fine."

"I hope so," Edgar said, panicking at the thought that he might not get along with his parents.

With every decision he made, Edgar was reminded he didn't know who he was. He didn't know if he was making choices the old Edgar would have made. But then he wondered, did it matter? If he could find a way to be happy with his new life, did he need to know everything about his past? Did his journey to uncover his secrets matter? Of course it did. He wanted to know the truth. About Jackson and Clara's deaths. His memory loss. All of it.

After a few more hours of driving, Liam became tired and they were both hungry, so they decided to stop for a late lunch at a diner right off the interstate in Shawnee, Oklahoma. They could relax for a bit and walk around to stretch their legs after being stuck in the car all day. At the diner, Liam ordered a grilled cheese with sautéed onions, five types of cheese, bacon, and tomatoes. Edgar ordered the nacho platter, which Liam ended up stealing more than a few chips from.

When they were both nearly done eating, the waitress came back and stood in front of their table awkwardly for a few seconds before asking, "Are these going to be separate bills?"

Liam made pointed eye contact with Edgar, then looked at the waitress. "Nope, I'll be paying for my meal and his," he said, pulling out his credit card and slapping it down on the table.

"Uh, okay," the waitress stammered, grabbing the credit card and hurrying away.

Liam shook his head. "Isn't it depressing how judgmental some people are, even in 2016?"

"What do you mean?" Edgar asked, with a blank look on his face.

"Oh, come on. She clearly didn't want to think about the possibility we could be a couple. Everyone in this state is homophobic."

Edgar's eyes narrowed. "Oh. I guess I didn't realize it was a problem."

Liam huffed sarcastically. "Of course it's a fucking problem. It's one of the reasons why I moved to Mexico and…" Liam trailed off.

Edgar realized Liam never talked about his past. All he mentioned was his move to Mexico for a fresh start. What was Liam hiding?

Edgar raised an eyebrow. "So…were you going to tell me what happened? Why *did* you leave the U.S.?"

"I hope she hurries up and brings my card back soon," Liam said quickly, drumming his fingers on the table. "We should leave as soon as possible, so we can drive a few more hours before it's too dark. I hate driving at night."

"Liam? Why are you avoiding the subject?"

Liam sighed, dragging his hand through his hair and resting his head in his hands on the table. "I promise I'll tell you. But I don't want to talk about it right now."

"Okay, fine. Tell me when you're ready."

Liam heaved a sigh of relief. "Thanks."

The waitress returned to their table with Liam's credit card and placed a pen gingerly on the table next to the check. She walked away without a word.

Liam signed the check, leaving a nice tip for the waitress despite her attitude, and they left the diner. Liam grabbed Edgar's hand when they were standing on the sidewalk and Edgar immediately jerked away.

"What are you doing?" Edgar said, madly looking around. "You're the one who said people are judgmental!"

Liam rolled his eyes. "I'm not afraid of some small-town hillbilly," he said in his best Southern drawl.

"Fine, but we're only holding hands," Edgar replied, grabbing Liam's hand before he could change his mind.

Edgar suggested they walk around town and explore for a little bit. They were both tired of being stuck in a car. Although they were behind schedule, Shawnee was a quaint little town with locally owned shops and restaurants downtown, a used bookstore, a thrift store, and a café. A paved trail started on the edge of town and led into the woods. They weren't sure how long it was but decided to try walking it until they became tired enough to turn around.

Edgar struggled to keep up with Liam. He was several inches shorter than Liam and couldn't match his stride. He couldn't remember the last time he exercised, and he was breathing heavily and sweating within minutes.

"Are you doing alright?" Liam asked, turning around to look at Edgar.

"I'm…fine," Edgar huffed, continuing to walk until he caught up with Liam. "We should have brought water bottles."

"It is hotter than I expected," Liam acknowledged. "I guess we can walk a little bit more and then go back to the car. Is that okay?"

"Sure, I could use the exercise. My legs are so stiff from sitting in the car all day."

Edgar stopped for a moment to catch his breath, sweat glistening on his forehead as he waited for his heart rate to slow down. Liam waited patiently for Edgar to be ready.

Edgar and Liam continued walking down the trail until the paved path turned to dirt. They were far enough into the woods now that they couldn't see town anymore. The trees were large, blocking most of the sun, covering them in blissful shade for a moment. They paused before starting down the dirt trail. A sudden explosive noise eerily reminiscent of a gunshot reverberated nearby.

"Did you hear a gunshot?" Edgar asked, wildly looking around.

"It's probably some rednecks shooting for target practice," Liam said with a grin. "Nothing to worry about."

Another gunshot echoed through the woods. It was closer. This time, it was followed by a gruff, male voice. "Get out of our fuckin' woods!" He yelled. "We don't welcome out-of-towners here and you're trespassin' on private property!"

Liam and Edgar turned to look at each other. A worn sign slightly off the trail, near where they stood said, "Private property: NO TRESPASSING." They both initially missed the sign and realized the danger immediately.

"Let's go!" Liam said as they saw a large man dressed in camouflage and tall black boots, holding a Remington 870, 12 gauge, running towards them.

"I said, get the fuck outta here!" The man yelled, charging towards Edgar and Liam.

"I'm sorry! We're leaving," Liam hollered back, pulling Edgar along.

Liam and Edgar ran back into town on the paved trail, both men running as fast as they could despite their exhaustion. Once they were out of the woods, they changed their pace to a fast walk until they stopped near the café they passed earlier.

"I think we're okay now. If he tries to come after us in town, there will be witnesses," Edgar said, wheezing.

Liam nodded. "Do you want to grab a coffee and a dessert from the café before we leave? I think we deserve it."

"That sounds amazing," Edgar agreed.

The camouflaged man stood at the edge of the woods. His eyes narrowed as he watched Edgar and Liam enter the café.

When they left the café fifteen minutes later with their coffee and pastries, the man was gone. But they returned to Liam's car to find all four tires with nails in them.

"It was the guy in the woods," Liam said, swiveling to check their surroundings. "I'm sure it was him."

"It might have been. But we're stranded here now and we need the tires patched. Hopefully there's an auto repair shop in this town that can tow your car and patch the tires quickly."

Liam groaned and kicked one of the tires with his scuffed black boot. Edgar wondered if he was paranoid or if everyone they encountered in the town so far was either terrified or disgusted by them.

Edgar whipped out his phone and searched for the nearest auto repair shop. He dialed the phone number. It was in town, but they closed at four and wouldn't be able to fix Liam's car tonight.

"What do we do now?" Edgar asked, helplessly leaning against the Dodge Challenger. "They said they would be here in twenty minutes to tow it, but we will be stuck here for tonight. We need to find a place to stay."

"Ugh, you're right. This road trip isn't going how I planned."

Edgar patted Liam's shoulder. "It will be okay."

Edgar found a cheap motel for the night and the auto mechanic was kind enough to drop them off after towing Liam's car. He promised he would patch the tires tomorrow morning.

The motel proved to be an upgrade from the previous night's stay. There was a mini fridge and microwave and the comforter on the bed wasn't covered in odd-looking stains, although the room smelled like cigarettes and must. They stocked up on snacks and alcohol from a nearby convenience store and settled into the motel room for the night. Neither of them thought exploring the town further was a good idea, since it seemed as if they were unwelcome visitors. It seemed safer to stay in the motel room. Besides, it was the perfect opportunity for Edgar and Liam to relax, watch a bad movie on cable, eat junk food, and get intoxicated.

Unfortunately, the only alcohol at the convenience store was cheap beer, so Edgar forced himself to drink it. By now, he knew enough of his food and drink preferences to realize he didn't like beer. Liam, however, didn't seem to be picky and drank the beer without complaint.

After they were both more than a few beers in and demolished a good amount of the snacks, Edgar nestled into the bed while they were watching *Bridesmaids*.

"I feel safe with you," he told Liam, slurring his words and turning to face him.

"Me too," Liam said, beaming and stroking Edgar's hair.

Edgar drifted off to sleep and Liam fell asleep shortly after. A few hours later, Edgar woke from a nightmare and startled Liam with his anguished cries.

"Edgar? What's wrong?"

"I had a nightmare," Edgar said, sitting up from his awkward sleeping position and realizing he fell asleep wearing his contacts. His eyes burned and the contacts felt stuck to his eyes. He didn't think he would be able to fall asleep again.

"About what?"

"It was—" Edgar started to say, unsure of how much he should reveal. He wasn't sure if his nightmares and visions were real. How could he find out? Was there a way he could prove he didn't kill Jackson and Clara? He didn't want to think about it because the more he did, the guiltier he felt.

"What?" Liam asked. "Do you want to try to go back to sleep?"

"No, I don't know if I can." Edgar leaned against the rough wooden headboard on the bed and adjusted the pillows behind his back. "Do you mind if I turn on the TV?"

"Okay, as long as the volume is low. I'm tired," Liam murmured, laying back down and attempting to make himself comfortable again. "Wake me up if you need me."

"Okay."

Edgar stayed up most of the night, watching mindless reality shows. He couldn't turn his mind off. It was impossible for him to calm down when he kept replaying the feeling of Jackson's lifeless body in his arms, the gaping hole in his head, and the blood cascading onto his shirt. On top of his racing thoughts, he still felt a little drunk and nauseous from all the beer, but he was finally able to drift into a restless sleep.

# Chapter 14: Delia

Delia brought her mom a meal from the hospital cafeteria, then she stopped by Oak Tree Assisted Living to grab several of her mom's outfits, her favorite pieces of jewelry, some books, and her toiletries, so she could feel more like herself. Delia decided to stay with her mom at the hospital until she was discharged, so she also stopped by her apartment to gather a few items she needed, including clothes, her laptop, and her notes about the Jackson Birkman case.

After her mom ate and laid dozing in the hospital bed, Delia pulled out her laptop and did a quick Google search for Edgar Peterson. Now several articles popped up regarding the American tourists who spotted Edgar near Lake Chapala, Mexico. There wasn't any new information. Each article regurgitated the same information worded in a slightly different way. There was plenty of speculation about what Edgar was doing in Mexico and who the mystery man was, but no one showed discernible proof of the truth. Edgar hadn't been spotted in months and no one knew what he had been up to since

Jackson's death. He was clearly hiding from the public, although whether that was to avoid being bombarded with questions by the press about Jackson's death or to suffer in silence from his guilty conscience, Delia wasn't sure.

After browsing the search results and reading through all the new articles she could find, Delia shut her laptop with a weary sigh. She was exhausted, worried about her mom, stressed about the hospital bills and medical expenses racking up by the day, and beginning to think there was no point in trying to find Edgar. No one believed her about Edgar's guilt during the initial investigation. Nothing changed since then. Edgar couldn't be connected to any crimes. Why couldn't she let it go and move on? The case was over; it had been for months and she needed to accept it. Besides, it was the worst time to leave the city. She had been selfish, but she knew she couldn't leave her mom now. An overwhelming sense of doubt crept in. Delia decided to call Jerry to update him about her mom's situation and express her skepticism about apprehending Edgar, so she went to the hospital parking lot.

"Hey, Delia!" Jerry said, cheerily answering the phone.

"Hi, Jerry. So, I have some bad news. Unfortunately, my mom had a stroke early this morning and I'm at the hospital with her right now. I haven't received an update from the doctor yet, so I'm not sure how severe the stroke was, but it has shaken me."

"Oh no…I'm sorry to hear about your mom. I hope she's able to make a full recovery."

"Thanks. I wanted to let you know because I'm not sure what to do about our flight to Minneapolis now. I know it's still two days away, but I don't know if I should leave my mom. She doesn't have anyone else to check on her, so if I leave now, she will be on her own."

"I completely understand. Spend time with your mom and take care of her. We can always cancel the flights and rebook them for a later date," Jerry said, reassuringly.

"Yeah. But my mom's stroke is making me reflect on my decisions. I'm reconsidering traveling to Minneapolis to find Edgar," Delia responded.

"Wow. Well, if that's what you want, then of course I'm fine with it, but take some time to think it through before we cancel our flights, okay?"

"I will. I should go, but thanks for being so understanding," Delia said.

"Of course. I can only imagine how rough that is to go through. Take care of yourself, Delia."

"You too," Delia said, hanging up.

Delia stood outside in the hospital parking lot trying to gather her thoughts. She needed a few minutes to herself. It was mid-afternoon and the parking lot was jammed full of cars. Patients and visitors strolled through the parking lot and down the sidewalk. The air felt fresh. A light breeze rustled Delia's red hair and she basked in the coolness of the outdoors. The hospital felt so stuffy and warm; the spring weather was a welcome reprieve.

Delia finally decided to go back inside but stopped in the hospital cafeteria to buy a cup of tea. She rarely drank caffeine and hated coffee, but she always craved a nice, steaming cup of hot tea, especially when her nerves were frazzled, and today definitely counted as one of those days. When she was back in her mom's hospital room, she discovered her mom was awake, but still lying in bed.

"Hey, Mom. How are you?" Delia asked, setting her tea on the small table in the room and sitting in the chair she occupied earlier by her mom's bedside.

"I'm okay. I keep drifting off. I can't seem to stay awake."

"It's okay. You've had a rough day. You can sleep if you want to. I'll be here," Delia reassured her.

"Okay," her mom said, closing her eyes and falling asleep again almost instantly.

A doctor knocked on the open hospital door and entered the room. "Hello, I'm Dr. Rutger," he greeted Delia, extending his hand for her to shake.

Delia shook his hand. "I'm Delia, Natalia's daughter."

Dr. Rutger glanced at Natalia's sleeping body. "Do you want to step into the hallway for a minute so we can talk?"

"Sure," Delia said, following him into the hallway as her heart pounded loudly in her ears. For a second, she was overcome with the intense urge to refuse to speak to him, to run away and avoid the bad news he might be about to deliver.

Dr. Rutger shut the door and they stepped into the hallway. "What have you been told so far about your mom's condition?"

"Um, the director of Oak Tree Assisted Living called me this morning and said she had a stroke. I missed the call because I was at work, but I came here as fast as I could after I heard what happened."

Dr. Rutger smiled kindly. "Your mom is a tough lady. Her stroke was in the brainstem. Unfortunately, this type of stroke can cause issues with the heart, vision problems, trouble with chewing and speaking, and could result in paralysis or a coma. Even when younger people have strokes, they don't survive without repercussions. Since your mom is in her sixties, it's harder for her body to recover from such a serious condition. She is almost completely paralyzed on the right side of her body now."

Delia sobbed and covered her mouth with her hand. "Is she going to be okay?"

"She has a small chance of recovering and learning to live with the right side of her body paralyzed, but the chance of recovery is slim due to the severity of the stroke," Dr. Rutger answered. "I'm sorry to break the news to you, Delia. I know this is difficult."

Delia sobbed again and this time she couldn't hold back her cries. She tried to hold herself together all day, hell, the past few months really, and now her world was crashing down on her. She covered her face in her hands and Dr. Rutger placed a gentle hand on her shoulder.

"If you need a few minutes, that's fine, but I do need to speak with you about your mom's options and what the remainder of her time here will be like."

"I think I need a minute to process this," Delia managed to choke out in between her sobs.

"Okay, I'll be back later. I'm sorry again, Delia."

Delia managed a nod of thanks and decided the best place to continue her mental breakdown was in her car, so she ran out to the parking lot and cried hysterically in her car for a solid twenty minutes. Afterwards, she felt cleansed, as if some of the pent up, negative emotions were dispelled from her body. She knew she would have to face the situation eventually, but she felt a little bit better for now.

Delia decided to drive to Shake Shack and went through the drive-through, ordering a burger, fries, and a large chocolate shake. Junk food was always her savior as a child. She was constantly teased in elementary school and middle school for being athletic, for not wearing dresses and bows, and for not caring if any boys liked her. It wasn't until she met Becca in high school that Delia finally found a friend she could be herself around. Even in high school, Becca never cared what people thought of her and always did whatever made her happy. Delia admired Becca's confidence and boldness and they had become fast friends.

Delia called Becca while she shoveled fries into her mouth and greedily slurped her chocolate shake. Faster than Delia would have thought possible, Becca showed up at Shake Shack and knocked on the driver's side window of Delia's car. Delia exited the car and Becca silently opened her arms for a hug. Neither of them was particularly affectionate women, but Delia accepted the hug and they wrapped their arms around each other. Delia felt safer and more loved than she had in months.

Becca insisted on going with Delia back to the hospital, so Becca followed Delia in her own car. They sat in the hospital room quietly chatting while Delia's mom lightly snored. Eventually, she woke up in a state of semi-confusion.

"Hi, girls. When did you arrive, Becca?" Delia's mom groggily croaked.

"Hi, Natalia. I came a little bit ago to keep Delia company while you were sleeping," Becca replied.

Delia stood from her chair and dragged it across the floor to sit closer to her mom. "Hey, Mom. How are you doing? Do you need anything?"

Delia's mom smacked her dried lips together. "Some water would be nice."

Becca immediately jumped up from her chair. "I'll go find some water for you."

Delia smiled in appreciation, knowing Becca volunteered so she could have a few minutes alone with her mom since she was finally awake.

"Do you want the TV on? Or maybe a book to read?"

"No, I think I'll just lay here. I've been awake for a little bit, but I was listening to you and Becca talk. You sounded like when you were high schoolers, giggling and whispering to each other."

Delia laughed. "You always told us we were being too loud when she slept over."

"Well, you always *were* too loud!" Her mom replied, joining her laughter.

Delia opened her mouth to say something but hesitated.

"What were you going to say, Delia?" She asked.

"Only that—never mind."

"Please tell me. I may not know exactly what's going on, but I'm in so much pain and I need a distraction."

"Okay. I talked to Dr. Rutger earlier and he told me having a severe stroke at your age is usually fatal. It's a miracle you survived."

"A miracle?" Her mom hoarsely laughed. "I would rather be dead right now, then maybe I could finally have some peace."

"Mom," Delia gasped. "You don't mean that."

Delia's mom tried to sit up in the bed, but struggled to position herself comfortably while only being able to use the left side of her body. "What? Where am I?" She frantically looked around the room, noticed the IV and tubes in her arm and realized she was lying in a hospital bed. "Why am I here?"

Delia gently patted her mom's hand. "It's okay, Mom. I'm here with you."

Delia's mom blinked several times and squinted at Delia. "Who are you? I don't know you," Delia's mom shrieked, yanking her hand away from Delia's. "Someone help me! There's a stranger in my room!" She screamed with surprising volume, considering her condition.

Delia slowly backed away from her mom, holding up her hands in a show of peace. A nurse came rushing in soon after.

"Is everything okay?" The nurse asked, adjusting Delia's mom's pillows and checking her fluid levels, vital signs, and the IV.

"No!" Delia's mom yelled hoarsely. "That woman is in here," she said, pointing at Delia.

"Mom, it's me, Delia," Delia said helplessly from across the room.

"She's not my daughter," Delia's mom whispered conspiratorially to the nurse. "My daughter is in high school. She gets straight As," she said proudly.

The nurse smiled at Delia. "That's great, Natalia," she responded to Delia's mom. "I'm sure she will be very successful someday."

"Oh, she will be," Delia's mom said. "She doesn't waste her time on boys and focuses on school. She's always studying. She's going to be great when she grows up," she said proudly, with every mom's confidence that their kid will be the one to change the world.

# Chapter 15: Edgar

The following day, Edgar and Liam were well-rested and ready to tackle their road trip. They were behind schedule, but arriving in Minneapolis one day later than they originally planned wasn't going to impact the outcome. The only reason they were in a hurry was because Edgar thought seeing and talking to his parents would help trigger his memories, or that talking to them would provide some clarity about his past.

"I guess we should call an Uber and go to the auto repair shop, then on our way out of town we can stop somewhere for gas and coffee," Liam suggested.

"Sounds good," Edgar agreed, helping Liam pack up their belongings for what felt like the hundredth time.

After the Uber dropped them off at the auto repair shop, Edgar knocked on the door. A "Closed" sign hung on the door and no one was around. Edgar knocked again, louder the second time, banging his knuckles hard against the door.

"Weird," Edgar said, finally giving up and stepping away from the door. "Do you think something happened? Maybe the mechanic slept in or had an emergency?"

"Hmm, I'm not sure. We can't wait around all day for him to show up. I'll try calling him." Liam pulled his cellphone out of his pocket and called the phone number listed on their website.

The phone rang endlessly, so Liam hung up and tried calling a second time, eventually deciding to leave a voicemail.

"Hey, this is Liam, the owner of the black Dodge Challenger you towed last night. My tires needed to be patched. I'm at your shop, but the "Closed" sign is on the door and it looks like no one is here. I thought my car would be ready by now. Please give me a call back when you receive this message. Thanks."

"Hopefully he calls back soon. Maybe he's in the back and didn't hear us knocking or the phone ringing," Edgar hypothesized.

"Yeah, maybe…" Liam trailed off, grabbing his suitcase and trying to peer inside the office of the repair shop.

Liam walked around the building, checking if any of the blinds were open or if he could find anything out of the ordinary. There was a silver Camry parked in the back.

"That must be the mechanic's car. I bet he's inside and he's ignoring us."

"Why would he ignore us?" Edgar asked, scrunching his eyebrows together in confusion.

"I'm not sure, unless he's trying to trap us here. We can't leave town without my car."

Edgar's eyes widened. "Okay, that sounds crazy. We're not in a horror movie. We're in a small town in Oklahoma!"

"I know, Edgar, but think about what has happened since we've been here. First, the waitress at the diner acted strange. Then, we encountered the camouflage guy with the gun in the woods. Next, we found out *all four* of the tires on my beautiful Challenger were stabbed with nails and now the mechanic hasn't fixed our car when he said he would?"

"Okay, but those could all be random coincidences. We have had bad luck since stopping here. That doesn't necessarily mean something is going on," Edgar said, glancing around the parking lot. "We do need to figure out if your car will be ready soon though, so we can continue our trip."

"You might be right. I'll try not to overthink the situation. Although we already checked out of the motel, so if we're forced to stay another night, then we'll have to check in again and book another room."

"I hope it doesn't come to that," Edgar responded, sighing and brushing his long, dark hair away from his face.

"Okay, so what do you think we should do?" Liam asked, pacing the nearly empty parking lot. "We have all of our stuff with us, so it doesn't make this easy."

"I know. Stop pacing. You're making me nervous."

"It helps me think," Liam shot back, glaring at Edgar and continuing his pacing.

The blinds in one of the windows opened a few inches and Edgar saw someone peer through the blinds.

"Hey!" Edgar yelled, pointing at the window. "Open the door!"

"What?" Liam asked, hurrying over to the window where Edgar pointed. "Did you see someone?"

"Yeah, I'm almost positive it was the mechanic. Let's try knocking on the door again."

Liam pounded on the steel door of the back entrance, the sound of his fist reverberating in the distance. "Open the fucking door."

"Hey, you don't have to swear," Edgar said. "We still need his help, you know."

"Sorry. *Please* open the door!" Liam yelled.

The back entrance opened slowly, the mechanic's face appearing as the door opened enough to reveal him. "Hey, what are you two doing here so early?"

Liam lunged towards the door when it opened enough and shoved his foot in between the door and the door frame, kicking it the rest of the way open. "We're here to pick up my car. You said it would be ready by now. We're from out of town and need the tires patched, so we can safely continue our road trip," Liam hissed, without taking a breath between words.

The mechanic pulled out a cigarette and a lighter from a pocket inside his overalls and lit the cigarette, taking a few puffs before blowing out the smoke towards Liam's face. "Yeah, well I usually don't open the shop until ten or so on weekdays. We don't get much business during the week and it's not worth it for me to be open all day. Sorry about the misunderstanding, but your car isn't ready."

Liam sighed exasperatedly and placed his hand on the door so the mechanic wouldn't try to shut it. "Look, I can pay extra for you to expedite the service if that's what you want, but as I said we're from out of town and we're kind of in a hurry…"

The mechanic took another puff of his cigarette and chortled loudly. "That's no problem of mine and I don't appreciate you implying I would run my business that way. I don't take bribes."

"How soon can you have the tires patched?" Liam asked, glancing at his phone to check the time. It was 9:05 a.m.

"Well, if I'm being honest with you, I have several other cars I'm supposed to service before yours and I'm not sure if I'll have time for your tires today."

Liam slammed his fist against the doorframe. "I'm trying to be understanding here, but we only stayed the night in this town because you promised the tires would be patched today."

"I'll try my best to get around to it soon. I have your phone number, so I'll give you a shout when your car is ready," the mechanic deadpanned, taking another drag of his cigarette.

"Fine. Please let me know as soon as possible if it won't be ready today because we will have to make arrangements to stay another night in a motel if that happens," Liam snapped back.

"Alrighty," the mechanic said.

"Come on, Edgar," Liam said, picking up his suitcase and walking towards Edgar who stood further away from the door.

Edgar and Liam carried their suitcases and walked around to the front of the building. Edgar's shoulder ached from his duffel bag hanging from it, so he switched the shoulder strap to his other shoulder for a moment of relief.

"What should we do now?" Edgar asked Liam, looking him directly in the eyes.

Liam put his arm around Edgar's shoulder. "I guess we should find somewhere to eat breakfast and coffee," he said, trying to smile.

"If nothing else, at least we're getting to spend some quality time together."

"Ah, yes, quality time being chased through the woods by a man with a gun and trapped in a town where apparently everyone wants to make our lives a living hell. My perfect idea of quality time with someone."

Liam's lips turned up in a partial smile as he and Edgar both began laughing.

"This entire road trip has been ridiculous so far," Liam said.

"So, coffee?" Edgar proposed, pulling out his phone to find a place they could hang out and hopefully eat breakfast, too. "I guess there's only one coffee shop in town. I'm assuming you don't want to go back to the diner we went to yesterday, unless you want to make a special request for that lovely waitress…"

Liam sneered. "Okay, the coffee shop it is then. I'll call an Uber. It's too far to walk there, especially with our bags. I wish we didn't have all of our stuff to carry around, then we could walk around town and maybe do some shopping. Then again, I'm not sure how safe 'exploring' this town is."

"Yeah, I think we stick to the coffee shop. They should have Wi-Fi, so we can check how many miles we have left until we reach Minneapolis and plan the rest of the trip. If we limit the rest of our stops, this little detour shouldn't set us back too much."

"Good idea," Liam said.

Since the town was so small, they waited nearly a half hour for the Uber to arrive. The Uber driver dropped them off directly in front of the coffee shop. As they jumped out of the car and gathered their suitcase and duffel bag, a car pulled up behind the Uber driver and impatiently started honking.

"Sorry!" Liam called, waving to the driver as he and Edgar ran to safety on the sidewalk.

They entered the coffee shop. Edgar carried their bags to a table while Liam waited in line to order. The coffee shop didn't have physical menus. Instead, their limited menu was written on the wall, which was painted like a chalkboard. After he received their drinks and breakfast, Liam carried the plastic tray over to the table where Edgar waited. He placed a coffee cup in front of Edgar and Edgar took a hesitant sip.

"You remembered," Edgar said, smiling and happily sipping his heavily sugared coffee.

"Of course. I don't know how I could forget after your reaction last time," Liam teased, taking a sip of his black iced coffee.

Liam pulled two bagels out of the brown paper bag on the plastic tray and slid one over to Edgar's side of the table. "I guess I should have asked what type of bagel you prefer, but I figured since you're a straightforward, honest guy, a plain bagel would be good."

Edgar smirked. "Hmm, that sounds about right," he said, peeling the wrapper off the bagel and taking a bite. "No cream cheese?"

Liam wrinkled his nose. "I'm not a fan of cream cheese."

"Interesting," Edgar said, taking a sip of his coffee. "I'm going to ask for some then."

Edgar asked for cream cheese at the counter where Liam had placed their order. They finished their bagels and coffee, but still hadn't heard from the mechanic.

"What should we do to kill time?" Edgar asked, picking up their trash and throwing it in the garbage bin near the door. "Should we hang out here in case your car is almost ready?"

"I'll call the auto repair shop and ask for an update. It would help if we knew if he's working on my car yet or if it's going to be awhile still."

Liam swiped through his phone to click on recent calls and touched the re-dial button for the auto repair shop.

"Hello?" The mechanic's gruff voice answered.

"Hey, it's Liam. I was wondering if you've gotten to my Dodge Challenger yet."

"Nope, I haven't had time for it."

Liam rolled his eyes at Edgar in frustration. "When will it be ready?"

"I'm not sure, probably by the end of the day, if not tomorrow," the mechanic answered.

"What?!" Liam exploded. "I need my car back by this afternoon! This is ridiculous. I've already been waiting a day and you haven't even started patching the tires. I'm sure it won't take long. Can't you stop whatever else you're working on and squeeze in my service request?"

Several patrons in the café turned to stare at Liam as his voice rose in anger, so Liam exited the café to continue his conversation outside. Edgar stayed in his seat at the table, sipping his coffee, when he unexpectedly became dizzy. The coffee shop was warm and his face flushed from the rush of heat. The once empty seat across from him was now occupied by Jackson.

"Please, Edgar," Jackson said. "There's no one else I can turn to. I'll pay you back as soon as I can. I promise this is the last time," Jackson pleaded.

"Okay," Edgar said. "But this is it." He slid a blank check across the table to Jackson. "Just fill in the amount you need like last time."

"You're the best friend a guy could have," Jackson said, grabbing the check, his face unfolding into a brilliant smile.

Edgar reached across the table to touch Jackson's hand, but his hand went through the empty air and Jackson's face fizzled out of existence.

"I'm still here," Jackson's voice whispered, now coming from directly behind Edgar, raising goosebumps on the back of his neck. "I'm always with you."

Edgar's vision blurred as he turned to the direction of Jackson's voice, frantically looking around the café, but Jackson wasn't there. Edgar was alone.

***

Edgar had seen Jackson appear several times now. He didn't believe in ghosts. He knew it was a manifestation of a deep-rooted desire to be able to see and talk to Jackson again. A sort of vision. It was only his imagination. Even if he couldn't remember his past, by now he knew how much he cared about Jackson and even losing his memory couldn't completely erase the feeling.

Liam came back into the café and slumped down in the chair across from Edgar, startling him out of his contemplation.

"This is fucking ridiculous, but I don't know when the tires are going to be patched and the mechanic refused to let me pick up my car and have it towed to a different auto repair place."

"Ugh," Edgar moaned, putting his head in his hands. "So, we're stuck here?"

"We could leave my car and fly to Minneapolis," Liam suggested halfheartedly.

"No, I know you don't want to leave your car. Plus, then we wouldn't have a way to explore when we're in Minnesota," Edgar said reasonably.

"True. What if I stayed here and you flew to Minneapolis by yourself? I can meet you there when my car is fixed. But it might take a little bit."

Edgar placed his hand on top of Liam's on the bistro table. "I don't want you to be stuck here by yourself."

"Well, is it much worse than us being stuck here together?"

"At least you're not alone. Besides, I'm not sure if I want to talk to my parents by myself. I don't remember them and I don't know what our relationship is like. I need you with me."

"Okay," Liam said, smiling and squeezing Edgar's hand. "So, we're staying here for now. I hope your parents are…nice."

"Me too."

"Do we dare leave this café to enter the crazy town? What else is nearby?" Liam asked.

"Hmm, I'm not sure. Let me Google it," Edgar said, picking up his phone from the bistro table in front of him.

Edgar Google searched the town and laughed at the results. "Well, this café is one of the top results for 'Things to do in Shawnee, Oklahoma.' There's also a park, a bar, and some antique shops." Edgar scrolled further down the page of results. "And not much else unless you're looking for a dentist or a dry cleaner."

"I guess we can check out a few of the antique shops. It sucks that we have to carry around all our bags though. I wish there was somewhere we could stow them for the day. If we hadn't checked out of the motel already, we could have kept our stuff there."

"It's fine. I would rather keep our stuff with us so there isn't a chance of it being stolen," Edgar said.

"To the antique shop then?" Liam asked, picking up his suitcase by the handle and putting the strap over his shoulder. "Now I wish I owned a suitcase with wheels."

Edgar picked up his duffel bag and they used Google Maps to navigate to the antique shop, although it wasn't a complicated journey. The town was so small that if they wandered for long enough, they would have stumbled across it eventually.

Edgar and Liam browsed both antique shops in town, taking their time looking at the old furniture, with Liam paying special attention to any records he found. Edgar found out Liam appreciated music and especially loved listening to his record player, which he left behind in Mexico. It was the hardest item for him to part with, but it would have been too difficult to safely transport, not to mention there wouldn't have been enough room in the car to also bring his enormous record collection along. Edgar assumed Liam would return to Lake Chapala at some point after their trip to Minneapolis– whether it was to retrieve the rest of his belongings from his apartment or to return for good, Edgar wasn't sure. He didn't think he would mind either way. He had enough to worry about without wondering what was going to happen between him and a guy he barely knew.

"I never saw your place in Lake Chapala," Edgar said suddenly as they exited the second antique shop. "You mentioned your record collection and I realized I never saw it."

"Yeah, I rented a small apartment. Nothing impressive. Trust me, you didn't miss out."

Edgar frowned. "Did you tell your landlord you were moving then? Are you planning on going back for the rest of your stuff?" He asked, breaking the rule he had set for himself.

Liam laughed and playfully tousled Edgar's long, dark hair. "Why do you have so many questions all of a sudden? I thought we had an agreement."

Edgar pulled away from Liam so he would stop messing up his hair and tried his best to pat it down. "Not really. We never discussed our plans after our road trip."

Liam stared at Edgar. "I thought we would find a place and move in together. Maybe near Minneapolis if you want to be close to your family. Or we could move to New York City if you would rather go back there. I'm fine with either city."

"What about your family? Don't you want to live near them? Where do they live?"

Liam picked at his nails and looked away. "They live in North Carolina and no, I don't particularly want to move back there."

"Do you have any siblings? Or is it just your parents?" Edgar was intrigued since he found out he was an only child. Although he didn't remember his childhood, he wondered what it was like to have siblings.

"I have a younger sister named Kate," Liam replied, tearing off a chunk of his nail. "She lives with my parents in Asheville."

Edgar noticed Liam ripping apart his fingernails. "Are you okay?"

"I'm fine. I don't like talking about them."

"When you were at the diner, you said you would tell me..." Edgar started to say but decided he didn't want to push Liam.

"I know what I said! I don't want to talk about it right now, okay? Drop it, Edgar."

"Okay," Edgar replied stiffly, becoming more certain he didn't have a future with Liam. That was fine with him. The more time they spent together, the more Edgar thought he was meant to be alone. Maybe it was because he lost Jackson. Maybe he would never fully heal from the loss.

Liam walked ahead of Edgar, his longer legs allowing for lengthier strides. Edgar slowed down even more and let him walk away, knowing that Liam was angry and it was best to let him cool off before he tried talking to him again. Besides, why did it matter if Liam wasn't close to his family or had a troubled past if Edgar didn't plan on staying with him? He didn't need to worry about it. Sure, Liam helped him, but did he need him anymore?

"Can you walk a little faster?" Liam yelled from further down the street, turning around to glare at Edgar.

"I was trying to give you space!" Edgar yelled back.

"Well, stop it. We're going to retrieve my car and then getting the fuck out of this town."

Edgar ran down the sidewalk to catch up with Liam, holding onto his heavy duffel bag and struggling with the weight of it. "Did the mechanic call you?" He asked in confusion as his breathing sped up.

"I thought you didn't know when your car would be ready for pick up."

"Nope, but we're going to the repair shop to make sure he fixes the tires and then we're leaving. I'm not staying another night here."

Edgar and Liam approached the auto repair shop. Liam set down his suitcase out front and gestured for Edgar to do the same.

"Come on," Liam said impatiently, shoving his hand in his pocket and walking towards the back of the shop where the garage was with the cars being fixed.

Edgar pushed himself to keep up with Liam and followed him to the back of the shop, wondering what Liam was thinking. He was angry and worked up, so he hoped Liam wasn't planning something stupid. The mechanic was in the garage working on a Chevy Impala when they stepped inside. He didn't hear them approach because Metallica blasted from an old, beaten-up looking stereo.

Liam walked over to the stereo and turned off the music to grab the mechanic's attention.

"Hey!" The mechanic yelled as soon as the music stopped. "What are you doing in here? This space is for employees only. You can wait inside the waiting room if you want to stay here."

Liam snickered nastily. "I don't think so. I've been waiting for my car much longer than I should have been. You're holding it hostage and we can't leave town without it."

"Sorry, but it's not ready. I've had a busy day. Yours is the next one on the list."

"I don't believe you," Liam said, stepping closer to the mechanic, his hands in his pockets. "You're going to patch the tires right now. I'll pay you and then we're leaving."

The mechanic laughed obnoxiously and wiped the sweat from his brow. "That's not how this works, buddy. I decide the schedule of repairs here by priority and patching tires doesn't make me a lot of money, so it's lower down on the list."

"I don't care how much money it costs. The way you do business is terrible. Isn't there someone else in charge here I can talk to?" Liam sniped.

"Nope, only me. The previous owner was sick. I think he had cancer, so he asked me to take over a few years ago. If you have any issues, then I'm the guy to talk to," the mechanic said.

"Look, I'm not asking for anything crazy. I just want my car back."

"Well, you're kind of being a dick about it, so back off and I'll get to it in a bit."

Liam shook his head back and forth in frustration. Edgar watched the scenario play out from the entrance of the garage. As he saw the way the mechanic treated Liam and how he insulted him, Edgar's fury intensified. He may not have a future with Liam, but he cared about him. He had patiently waited to see what would happen, but he saw an opening and decided to take it.

Edgar lunged forward, picking up a large wrench from inside the garage and striking the mechanic in the forehead with it as hard as he could. The mechanic froze in shock and fear, so he fell to the ground as Edgar struck him in the head with the wrench a second time. By the time Edgar pulled back his arm to hit the mechanic a third time, Liam had sprung forward and roughly grabbed Edgar's arm to stop him.

"What are you doing?" Liam screeched, taking the wrench forcefully from Edgar's hand and taking a few steps away from him.

Edgar's chest heaved as he stared at the mechanic lying unconscious on the concrete. He looked so helpless, lying on the ground unable to move or protect himself. He kicked the mechanic in the stomach a few times, enjoying the feeling as his shoe made contact with the fat in the man's stomach. Edgar felt power surge through his body, the overwhelmingly familiar power of taking someone down. He thought he had killed before, but now he was certain. Edgar didn't want to go back to the way things were. He was done acting passive, meek, going along with whatever Liam wanted. He wasn't meant to live his life that way. Edgar knew he was meant for greatness.

Liam slowly backed away from Edgar, holding the wrench. "What did you do?" He said softly, looking back and forth between Edgar and the unconscious mechanic.

"I did what I had to. He wasn't treating you right," Edgar responded, steeling himself and looking Liam squarely in the eyes. "Besides, I know you have a pocketknife in your pocket that you were clenching the entire time you were talking to him. You were waiting for an excuse to use it, but you were too scared."

Liam fiddled with the pocketknife in his pocket and put the wrench in his other pocket. "Okay, we will take the wrench with us so there isn't any evidence. The mechanic knows my first name, my phone number, my car's make and model, and my license plate number. If we leave my car here and leave town, we should be fine."

A smile creeped slowly across Edgar's entire face, the type of genuine smile that spread all the way to his eyes. Jackson appeared next to him, shaking his blood-soaked head in disapproval.

"Edgar, I thought you were better than this. I thought you were trying to be a good person and redeem yourself for your past sins," Jackson said.

Edgar turned to Jackson. "Redemption for what? I have amnesia, remember?"

Liam looked at Edgar, who appeared to be talking to himself, with apprehension. "Edgar?"

Edgar ignored Liam. "I know why you're here," he said to Jackson. "You're trying to make me feel guilty. It's not going to work. I don't have my memories back yet, but once I do, everything will make sense again."

"What?" Liam asked, looking around and ferociously ripping at his fingernails.

"Nothing," Edgar said.

Jackson floated closer to Edgar, hovering several inches above the ground. The smell of rotting flesh was pungent so close to Edgar's face. "Don't lose the one person you care about, Edgar. It almost killed you when you lost me. Don't make the same mistake this time. You have a second chance."

"Shut up!" Edgar screamed as whatever form Jackson had taken dissipated.

"Edgar, despite whatever is going on with you, we need to leave," Liam said worriedly. "An employee or another customer is going to come here eventually and they'll find the mechanic. I don't want them to find us with him."

Edgar tried to regain his composure. Liam had witnessed him talking to Jackson several times now, although to Liam it seemed as if

Edgar talked to himself and carried on a full conversation. What did it mean that he kept seeing Jackson? Was he going crazy?

"Edgar?" Liam said in a small voice, looking around the garage. "Is he…dead?"

Edgar glanced down at the body. It didn't look like the man's chest was moving. He leaned down close to his face but didn't hear any breathing.

"No," Edgar lied. "It sounds like he's breathing. He'll be fine." Edgar stood from his position on the floor, picked up his duffel bag near the garage entrance, and started walking away, only looking back when he realized Liam still stood in the garage, unmoving.

"Liam, are you coming? You're right—we need to leave."

Liam nodded, slowly forcing himself to pick up his own suitcase and follow Edgar out of the garage. "What are we going to do without my car?"

Edgar paused thoughtfully for a moment, tucking his long hair behind his ears. "I saw a bus station on the edge of town. We can take the bus until we reach Missouri and then hitchhike. Or we could fly the rest of the way, but I doubt there's an airport nearby since this town is so small."

"Okay, we can take the bus then," Liam agreed, following Edgar as he walked away from the auto repair shop and away from the mechanic.

Edgar noticed Liam carefully avoid walking too close to the mechanic's body. He wondered what Liam thought. Did he know he was lying?

# Chapter 16: Delia

Delia watched the news as she sat in her mom's hospital room. A headline flashed across the TV that read "Owner Found Dead in Auto Repair Shop in Shawnee, OK." Delia shuddered as the reporter explained how the owner's body was found by another employee of the repair shop. The owner's body was sprawled out on the concrete floor in the repair garage, with gouges in his head and a pool of blood near his body. The employee immediately called an ambulance, but the owner was already dead when he found him. The employee was being treated as a suspect because the police didn't have any other leads yet.

Seeing this horrific news story made Delia contemplate the Jackson Birkman case again. It seemed to be another case where the murderer was potentially going to get away with killing. Delia wondered what Edgar was doing right now and whether he had killed since then. She wondered if murderers could become rehabilitated if they went to prison and served a long enough sentence. Did murderers feel guilty after killing? Or did they try to justify it to themselves? Was it possible to feel remorse after committing such an atrocious act? Delia wasn't sure how to answer any of her questions, but she continued to ponder them as her mom snored loudly in the hospital bed.

Delia talked to Becca about everything on her mind: her mom's stroke, the Alzheimer's, quitting her job, the potential trip to Minneapolis, and leaving her mom alone in the hospital. Becca consoled her by promising to be available if her mom needed help while Delia was out of town. She said she would call her immediately if something happened. Becca also suggested Delia could always fly back to New York if necessary. Edgar would still be out there somewhere and she could always try to find him later.

After a few more hours of shifting around in the uncomfortable hospital chair, unsuccessfully trying to soothe her aching back, Delia decided she needed some fresh air. As she exited the hospital, an inky blackness crept across the sky. She stared, watching the light disappear, debating where she should go. She drove home and stayed the night in her apartment. Maybe a decent night of sleep in her comfy, queen-sized bed would help her better tackle whatever she had to deal with tomorrow. Besides, she didn't want to leave Lily alone in her apartment for too long.

Delia tossed and turned in her bed for most of the night. She finally fell asleep around 4:00 a.m. and slept until noon. When she woke up, she nearly jumped out of bed when she checked her phone and saw the time. Multiple missed texts and phone calls—a few from Becca checking on her, one from Will saying he was thinking of her, and one from Jerry asking for her address. She sent thanks to Becca and Will and texted Jerry back, wondering why he wanted her address. She received a response from Jerry almost immediately. He had the day off and wanted to stop by with breakfast.

Delia realized she was still wearing her jeans and long-sleeved blouse from yesterday and hadn't brushed her teeth before falling asleep. She took off her clothes and threw them towards her laundry hamper, deciding a shower was necessary. Taking a hot shower usually made her feel better. If nothing else, she would be refreshed and clean. After her shower, Delia threw on a different pair of jeans and one of her favorite burgundy sweaters, then brushed the knots out of her red hair. While Delia blow dried her hair, the doorbell rang.

"Hey, Jerry," Delia said, opening the door.

Jerry smiled brightly, his brown eyes crinkling. "Hey, Delia. I brought bagels," he said, holding up a large stuffed paper bag.

"Thank you, that's so nice. You didn't have to do this," Delia said.

"It was nothing. Besides, I wanted to check on you," Jerry responded, walking into the tiny kitchen where his large frame seemed to take up most of the space.

Jerry set the bag on the counter. "I wasn't sure what kind of bagels you liked, so I asked the woman at the counter to give me one of every kind."

Delia laughed. "Wow, so I guess I have options," she said, pulling the bagels out of the bag one by one and deciding on a bagel covered in cheese.

"Okay, then I'll take the everything bagel," Jerry said. "Don't worry; there's cream cheese at the bottom of the bag too."

Delia and Jerry sat at the tiny bistro table in her kitchen, munching on their bagels in silence.

"I would have brought coffee too, but I remembered you didn't drink it," Jerry said, shoving the last chunk of bagel into his mouth.

"Thanks for remembering. I can make some tea if you want?"

"No thanks. I don't drink tea."

Delia ate slowly, so she nibbled on her bagel while Jerry sat next to her awkwardly waiting for her to finish.

"You said you have the day off?" Delia asked after her bagel was gone.

"Yeah, the nice part about being a private detective is that I make my own schedule and can decide which days I want to work. I work long hours on most days, but every once in a while, I let myself have a break."

"I understand. I recently quit my job, but I always volunteered to work on nights and weekends or pick up extra shifts."

"Where were you working?" Jerry asked.

"As a security guard at The Fox Luxury Apartments," Delia answered.

"Why did you quit? That doesn't sound so bad."

Delia sighed as she thought about the multitude of reasons she left the job. "It's complicated."

"Most things in life usually are."

"I needed a new job after I quit the police force. I didn't want a dangerous job and the pay was okay."

"Ah. You needed a change, but it wasn't the right type of change. Maybe you needed to work there to better understand what you want from a career," Jerry said.

Delia paused thoughtfully. "You might be right. Working as a security guard made me realize that wasn't the right fit for me either. In fact, I feel even more lost than I did a few months ago."

"It's okay to feel lost sometimes," Jerry said, smiling kindly. "It happens to all of us."

"It's been difficult to deal with everything on my own and not have someone to lean on when I can't handle it."

"I understand. I've been alone for most of my life, so I know how lonely it can be. It's important to surround yourself with good friends and make them your family."

"You're right. And I do have a few close friends, Becca and her husband, Joel. I've known them since high school, so they understand me and they've always been there for me. I know I'm lucky to have them in my life," Delia said.

Jerry nodded. "I've drifted away from most of my friends. It's difficult to stay close to anyone when you're constantly chasing cases and traveling across the country. Working long hours doesn't help either."

Delia walked over to the stove to boil water for a pot of tea. "Are you sure you don't want some tea? I drink it every day and feel like I can't start my day without it."

Jerry shook his head good-naturedly. "No thanks, I don't like tea."

Delia watched the water begin to bubble and pulled out a tea bag from her organized collection in the cupboard. She owned dozens of teas to choose from, but a chocolate mint black tea blend was one of her favorites.

"Well, what are your plans for the day?" Jerry asked.

Delia paused as she watched the tea bag steeping in the water. "I'm going to spend the day with my mom at the hospital. I need to check on her."

Delia pulled the tea bag out of the tea pot and threw it in the trash can. It had steeped long enough. She spooned honey into her mug and poured the tea over it, stirring the honey until it dissolved, and joined Jerry at the tiny kitchen table again.

"Are your parents still alive?" Delia asked abruptly, clenching her steaming mug of tea in both hands.

Jerry hesitated and scratched his mustache. "My dad committed suicide when I was eight, so my mom raised me. It's still difficult to talk about sometimes. My mom remarried when I was eighteen, after I moved out. I don't worry about her as much as I would if she lived by herself. I know my stepdad will take care of her. He's a good person. He never tried to be a dad to me; he was always more of a friend, which was what I needed."

Delia loosened her grip on her mug and reached one hand across the table to place it lightly on top of Jerry's hand. "I'm so sorry, Jerry," she said as Jerry gently squeezed her hand. "I can't imagine going through that, especially at such a young age."

"It wasn't easy, but I tried to be there for my mom as best I could. I helped around the house with chores and I learned how to cook. I got good grades and stayed out of trouble, so she didn't have to worry about me. I started working as soon as I was old enough, so I could help pay the bills. First, I mowed lawns in the summer, shoveled driveways in the winter, odd jobs for the neighbors. Eventually, I had a nice little business going. After I graduated from high school, I knew I wanted to become independent and move out, so I enrolled in the police academy. I enjoyed being a police officer for years, but I knew it wasn't exactly what I wanted to do."

"I'm sure your mom appreciated your help. It sounds like you had an entrepreneurial spirit from a young age, so it makes sense you ended up working for yourself," Delia said, taking a sip of her chocolate mint tea that was finally starting to cool off.

"I tried my best," Jerry responded, then faltered before continuing. "How is your mom doing, by the way?"

Delia took another small sip of her tea before answering. "She's more confused every day. It's so hard to watch, especially on days like yesterday." Delia set down the mug. "It was the first time she didn't recognize me," she said in a small voice.

"Oh no. I'm sorry, Delia. Let me know when you want me to leave, so you can go see her."

"I'm honestly dreading going back to the hospital today because I don't know if she will be any more cognizant or if her days of having her memory are over," Delia said.

Jerry noisily pushed back his chair, which screeched across the tile floors and walked around the table to Delia. "Do you want a hug?" He asked, holding out his arms and grinning.

"Sure, why not?" Delia responded, accepting Jerry's hug and wrapping her arms around him.

Delia pulled away as soon as the embrace started to feel too long and Jerry smiled at her as she backed away.

"Well, uh, I should go see my mom. It was nice seeing you though. Thanks again for the bagel."

Jerry gathered up the leftover bagels and headed towards the door. "No problem. Call me anytime you need someone to talk to. I'm looking forward to our future trip to Minneapolis."

"Me too," Delia said as Jerry shut the door and left.

Delia spent the rest of the day at the hospital with her mom, who slept the entire time. Dr. Rutger came to check on her and Delia asked for an update about her mom's health and mental state. Unfortunately, it wasn't good news. Dr. Rutger told Delia that her mom didn't seem to know who or where she was. When he tried explaining the situation to her, she became violent, so they were forced to sedate her again.

Delia sat in her mom's hospital room, watching bad soap operas on TV and trying not to think about what would happen after her mom was gone. She would have to arrange the funeral, notify their friends and family, and deal with all the associated expenses. The worst part, though, would be the grieving process. Delia wished she could skip to the part when she would feel normal again, but she knew it was impossible.

# Chapter 17: Edgar

Edgar and Liam arrived in Minneapolis two days later. They rode a bus through Oklahoma, then a nice older man picked them up in Iowa, before they hitchhiked the rest of the way to Edgar's parent's house. They stood outside of what was apparently Edgar's childhood home, a small red brick house with a tiny front porch, a driveway with cracks in the concrete that needed to be repaired, a lawn covered in spring frost, and several large oak trees.

Liam looked at Edgar, who waged an inner battle about ringing the doorbell and "meeting" his parents. "Ready?" Liam asked, placing his hand gently on Edgar's back and nudging him closer to the front door.

Edgar smiled nervously. "I think so. I'm glad I'm not alone."

Edgar took the final steps to the front door and pressed the doorbell. He heard the faint *ding dong ding dong* echoing throughout the house and tried to be patient as he waited for someone to answer the door. He rocked back and forth on his heels in anticipation.

A woman with bright green eyes and curly, dark red hair that appeared box-dyed, wearing an oversized sweater that wasn't flattering on her large frame, answered the door. "Hello…?" She said at first, then screamed, "EDGAR!" She jumped forward and embraced him tightly in her arms, as she began to sob.

Edgar hugged her back, but became uncomfortable quickly and gently pushed her away. "Are you my mom?" He asked.

The redheaded woman laughed, wiping tears from her eyes. "What kind of a question is that, silly? Of course I am! Oh, I'm so glad to see you. I've thought about you so much, especially lately." Her Minnesotan accent wasn't apparent at first, but it was now.

"Can we come inside?" Edgar asked.

"Oh…" Edgar's mom said, noticing Liam for the first time. "Who are you?" She asked, side-eyeing him.

"I'm Liam, Edgar's…friend," Liam said, shaking Edgar's mom's hand politely.

"Nice to meet you, Liam. I'm Edgar's mom, but you can call me Barbara. Or Barb! It used to drive me crazy, but I don't mind as much now that I'm older."

Barbara opened the door widely, gesturing for them to enter the house. "Come in, come in. I just brewed some coffee for myself, but I can make more. I always enjoy a nice, little mug of coffee in the afternoon."

"Coffee would be great, thanks," Liam said, glancing at Edgar who had remained silent since they entered the house.

Although small, the house was cozy and inviting. The entrance opened into a family room with hardwood floors and tan walls stuffed full of furniture, including several couches, a leather recliner, an antique coffee table, and a moderately sized TV mounted above a blazing electric fireplace. Bookshelves lined every wall from floor to ceiling. There were stacks of books on the floor throughout the room and scattered across the coffee table in front of one of the couches.

"Sit anywhere," Barbara said, walking to the kitchen to brew more coffee.

Edgar and Liam sat on one of the couches, both looking around the room. Edgar noticed a distinct lack of family photos on the walls and bookshelves, but maybe his parents kept them in another room. Barbara returned a few minutes later with three steaming mugs of coffee.

"Thanks," Edgar said, taking one of the mugs from Barbara.

"You betcha," Barbara responded. "Cream and sugar?" She asked Liam. "I know you always use sugar in yours," she said, smiling at Edgar.

Liam took a hesitant sip of the black coffee and pursed his lips in distaste. It was unlike any coffee he had ever tasted. "Cream and sugar would be nice."

Barbara laughed. "Edgar likes his coffee the same as you." She returned to the kitchen to retrieve cream and sugar for Liam, then came back into the family room and claimed the leather recliner.

Edgar perked up in his seat. "Where is Dad?"

Barbara frowned. "We don't need to talk about him right now. What are you doing here, Edgar? I was so shocked when I saw you on the doorstep, but now that I've had a few minutes to think about it…it's been so long. Why did you decide to visit after all these years?"

Edgar sipped his coffee. "I don't understand. How long has it been since I last saw you and Dad?"

Barbara glanced at Edgar and looked at Liam. "Oofda. You know exactly how long it's been since…the day you told us. You know."

"Mom," Edgar said, the word feeling foreign. "A few months ago, I woke up in Lake Chapala, Mexico with no memory of who I was or how I ended up there. I think I have amnesia. I still don't have my memories back, but after I found out I was an actor on a popular TV show I was able to find some information about my life. I tracked down this address. But I don't remember you. Why haven't we seen each other in years? What happened?"

"Oh, Edgar," Barbara said, cradling her coffee mug in her large hands. "You really don't remember? We can have a fresh start," she said, smiling with tears glistening in her green eyes.

"But I want to remember. I need to know what happened. That's why I came here," Edgar said, becoming agitated.

"Calm down, Edgar. It's not worth making a fuss about it. All that matters is you're here now, although I suppose you can't catch me up on what's happened in your life the past ten years. I know about Jackson, of course. I was struck with grief when I heard. He was always such a good friend to you," Barbara rambled, rocking back in her chair.

"Can you tell me about Jackson?" Edgar asked, sitting on the edge of the couch and leaning forward earnestly.

Liam's eyes narrowed. He didn't like the way Edgar looked when he said Jackson's name.

"Oh yah. You two became friends when you were in preschool. Your dad and I are both writers. Back then, neither of us were successful, so your dad took a corporate job to make some money. He met Jackson's dad, Rick, while he worked there and became quite close to him. Since you and Jackson were the same age, I arranged a play date with Rick's wife, Susan, and it went well the first time. So, Rick and Susan would come over for dinner or drinks once a week and you and Jackson would play. I wondered if you two would grow apart when you were older, but I guess you stayed close all those years," Barbara explained.

"Wow. I can't believe I've known him since preschool."

"You had a long friendship that you should be grateful for. Of course, his death was tragic, but some people never have a friendship like yours and Jackson's, so you should consider yourself lucky you had his companionship for so long," Barbara said, smiling sadly.

"I wish I could remember him," Edgar said wistfully.

Barbara loudly slurped her coffee. "How did you lose your memories?"

"I don't know. The first thing I remember is waking up in Lake Chapala, with no idea about where I was or who I was. I still don't know much more than I did then. I thought maybe coming here to talk to you and dad would help," Edgar said.

Barbara set down her nearly empty coffee mug on the side table. A snow-white cat with one green eye and one blue eye slinked out of the kitchen and towards the family room, but ran back into the kitchen when she spotted strangers in her house. "That's Kitty. We adopted her after you moved out. I'll try my best to help you, Edgar, but I'm afraid your dad won't be much help."

Edgar frowned. "Where is dad? What's wrong?"

Barbara downed the rest of her coffee in a final gulp and slammed the mug back down on the table. "He's in the hospital. He has lung cancer. Who would have thought all those years of smoking would finally catch up to him?" She said sarcastically and gestured at the dirty ashtray and pile of cigarette butts on the coffee table.

"I'm sorry…" Edgar said, then realized he apologized for his dad having lung cancer. He didn't know what emotion to feel, a combination of sadness that his dad was dying, guilt that he didn't care as much as he should, and regret that he wouldn't have the chance to know his dad.

Barbara smiled sweetly. "I'm so glad we have this opportunity to start over. We can get to know each other again. After what happened, I didn't think you would ever speak to us again. I know it was your dad's fault, but I didn't exactly stop him…"

"Can you please tell us what happened?" Liam asked, speaking for the first time in several minutes. "We came here so Edgar could spend some time with his family and learn about his past. Whatever happened, the good and the bad, he wants to know the truth."

Barbara sighed and shook her head. "Yah. Well, it was so long ago. Ten years. It hardly matters now since you're here."

Edgar sipped his coffee that was now lukewarm and set it back on the coffee table, half-finished. The coffee wasn't very good; it was probably instant coffee, so even drinking it with cream and sugar proved difficult.

"Ten years ago… That's a long time for us to not talk. Did we have an argument? What happened?" Edgar asked curiously.

Barbara waved him off, annoyed at his persistence, and picked up her coffee mug, with the recliner creaking as she stood. "I'm going to bring the mugs into the kitchen. Are you two done?"

Edgar and Liam both nodded and handed their mugs to Barbara.

"I don't like dishes sitting out," Barbara said loudly from the kitchen as she rinsed the mugs. "I prefer the house to be spotless."

Liam made eye contact with Edgar and laughed quietly at the irony. Books lined every available surface in the family room, the ashtray was full of cigarette butts, and cat hair permanently embedded into the furniture and the large, teal rug in the middle of the room.

Barbara came back into the room and wearily sat in the recliner once again, staring out the window at the sky. "It will be dark in a few hours. Do you need a place to stay, Edgar?"

"That would be great if you have the room. Thank you. We would love to stay here," Edgar answered hopefully.

Barbara stared at Liam, who sat a respectable distance from Edgar and avoided touching him, although they were on the same couch. "Edgar, you can sleep in your old room and Liam can have the couch. It's quite comfy; I nap on it sometimes."

Liam nodded. "Thanks, Barbara. We appreciate the hospitality."

Edgar stood up from the couch. "I'm hungry. Do you want us to go pick up dinner?" Then, Edgar remembered what happened to Liam's car and that they didn't have a method of transportation. "Well, we don't have a car, but we could order food online and have it delivered?"

"Oh no, that's not necessary," Barbara said, standing also. "I have plenty of food here. I can make a nice dinner for all of us."

"I'll help you cook as a thank you for letting us stay here," Edgar said.

"I'll help too. I'm a much better cook than Edgar," Liam said, laughing.

Edgar and Liam followed Barbara into the tiny, outdated kitchen with white appliances, white linoleum flooring, and a large, oval shaped kitchen table with four matching wooden chairs that had seen better days. The tops of the tan cabinets were full of ceramic roosters in an assortment of shapes and sizes.

"How did you two meet?" Barbara asked, pulling out ingredients from the pantry and opening the fridge to scour the shelves for food.

Liam smiled broadly. "I worked as a bartender at a restaurant and tequila bar in Lake Chapala. Edgar wandered in one day. He looked terrible. His hair was stringy and dirty. He had a wound on his head with dried blood on it. He looked like he had slept in his clothes for days. He carried a duffel bag with him. It took me awhile before I recognized him. He came up to the bar and ordered a meal and a few drinks. While I talked to him, I realized he was an actor on *Dispatching David...*" Liam trailed off, looking anxiously at Edgar.

"Oh yah, of course you recognized him from the show," Barbara said proudly. "Your dad refused to watch it, but I watched it every week, especially when you were starring in an episode."

Edgar clenched his fists tightly and set down the ground beef. "You knew who I was back then," he said accusingly, glaring at Liam, the suppressed anger returning.

"No, I told you—I didn't know at first. You looked so different. I wasn't sure if it was you. And it didn't make sense that you would be in Lake Chapala, so I thought I imagined it. Why would a famous actor from an award-winning American TV show be at a random restaurant in Mexico?" Liam replied, laughing nervously and taking a step closer to Edgar.

"You *knew* but you didn't tell me," Edgar said, moving closer to Liam. "I spent weeks trying to piece together any information I could find about my past, who I was, where I was from. But you hid it from me like a fucking snake."

Barbara gasped and covered her mouth. "Dontcha know, there's no need for foul language here, Edgar! I know you use it all the time on your TV show, but I won't allow it in this house."

"*And you,*" Edgar said, turning to his mom and pointing his finger at her. "I know something terrible must have happened between us, since you won't tell me. You think you can erase whatever you did? If I went ten years without speaking to you and dad, I can only imagine what terrible thing you must have done."

"Edgar, please, calm down. I'll explain it all. We'll make dinner and eat, then we can talk later, okay?" Barbara said.

"Your mom is right, Edgar. We don't need to fight. We will talk it out after dinner. I think we're both hungry and tired from the long trip," Liam said.

Edgar nodded slowly. "Okay, take her side, Liam. I thought you were supposed to be my partner."

"*I am,*" Liam said pleadingly, looking at Edgar with his green, almond-shaped eyes appearing bigger than usual.

"You have been lying to me since we met. I could have known who I was sooner. I could have come here to meet my parents months ago if I knew where they lived. Maybe then I could have seen my dad in time, before he was so sick…" Edgar said wistfully.

"Your dad has been sick for quite some time. It wouldn't have made much of a difference if you visited a few months ago. Besides, you can still visit him in the hospital. He isn't in the best mental state, but I'm sure he would be happy to see you," Barbara said.

Liam took a final step towards Edgar, wrapping his arms tightly around Edgar in an embrace. "Edgar, please, there's no need to become agitated. We can talk about whatever you want and I promise I'll explain everything. Even my past, what happened to make me move to Mexico."

Edgar softened, accepting the hug, but pulled away after a minute. Barbara stared at the two men tightly embracing and wrinkled her nose.

"Okay, that's enough," Barbara said, although Edgar had already backed away from Liam.

Edgar stared at his mom, the puzzle pieces connecting. He still didn't remember exactly what happened with his parents ten years ago, but after spending a few hours with Barbara and seeing how she acted towards him and Liam together and how she was clearly uncomfortable with them showing any affection, he could guess what happened.

"What happened ten years ago…" Edgar started, trying to figure out how to word his question, then deciding to ask outright. "Did it have something to do with me being gay?"

Barbara's face whitened and she gasped, looking back and forth between Edgar and Liam. "I never wanted you to leave. I didn't mean for it to go so far. I was willing to give you a chance to explain your feelings, so we could understand what you were going through. It came as a shock to us. But, your dad…he didn't want to hear about it. He said you were no longer a member of the family if that was the choice you were making," Barbara said, sobbing. "He has always been so set in his ways. He's so old-fashioned. I wanted to stop him from kicking you out, but I wasn't strong enough to stand up to him back then."

Edgar's face hardened as Barbara explained what happened to cause a rift in their family. At least now he knew. It wasn't his fault that his parents cast him out of their family. Edgar revealed his true self to his parents and they hadn't accepted him. What kind of parent did that?

"Did you ever tell him he was wrong?" Edgar asked, crossing his arms over his chest. "Because if you didn't, then you're as bad as he is."

Tears streamed down Barbara's face as she reached out her hands to Edgar. "It's been the one real regret of my life, losing you. I've always loved you, no matter what you did. You were such a bright child. I always knew you would turn your life around."

"What do you mean, 'turn my life around?'" Edgar questioned. How many secrets were buried in his past?

"Oh, well, I only meant that when you were a kid you never had many close friends. I used to worry about what would happen to you when you were older. I was so happy when you met Jackson and he stayed friends with you all those years," Barbara replied.

"Okay," Edgar said, looking around the kitchen. "I haven't seen any family photos in the house. You don't keep any of them out?"

Barbara exhaled wearily. "I don't have many left. After the falling out, your dad cut most of them up and threw them away. I tried to salvage what I could. I always hoped you would forgive us and come back someday."

"Can I see them?" Edgar asked eagerly. "Maybe looking at old photos will help trigger my memory. I thought coming here would help me remember my past, but so far it hasn't."

"Well, okay. I'll have to go find them. They're in my bedroom somewhere, probably packed away in the closet. It still made me sad to look at them and remember how our lives used to be, back when we were a happy family," Barbara said.

"Which bedroom is yours?" Edgar asked, exiting the kitchen and entering the hallway where he assumed the bedrooms were. "I can look for the photos."

"No, no, that's okay," Barbara said, hurriedly blocking the path to the hallway. "You and Liam can continue cooking dinner and I'll go find them."

"Oh. Okay." Edgar walked back to the kitchen. His mom hadn't mentioned what she planned on cooking for dinner, but he and Liam would figure it out.

"I guess we're on kitchen duty," Liam said, grinning at Edgar as he entered the kitchen again.

Edgar scowled. "I'm still upset with you. I'm not letting it go until you tell me everything."

Liam started to speak, but Edgar stopped him.

"Not right now. We can talk later. Help me with dinner," Edgar said, dumping the ground beef into a skillet on the stove and finding tortillas in the pantry. "We can make tacos. Even I can't screw that up."

"Okay," Liam said softly, gathering the other ingredients. "But you can't be mad at me forever. I didn't mean to hurt you."

"I don't want to talk about it now," Edgar said as he chopped the ground beef into tiny pieces. The aroma of meat sizzling in the skillet filled the kitchen.

"I promise I only have your best interests at heart," Liam said, wrapping his arms around Edgar's waist and pulling him close.

Barbara walked into the kitchen and dropped the photo album in her hands. "Wh-what on Earth are you doing to my son?" She screamed at Liam.

Edgar abruptly felt warm and fuzzy. His face flushed and he saw black spots dancing in front of him. Jackson appeared next to him, his blood-soaked head shaking back and forth in irritation.

"Why is your mom acting weird when she sees you with a man? She may say she loves you and wants to move on from what happened, but she still sees you as a monster," Jackson said.

"Shut up," Edgar muttered.

Jackson laughed and leaned against the kitchen counter. "Do you remember all those sleepovers we had? When we were young, we used to sleep in the same bed. Remember when we were too old to sleep together and your dad came in yelling at us to act like men? 'Men aren't meant to sleep together,' he said. I bet you secretly liked it, sleeping next to my body, curled up against me. Do you remember, Edgar?" Jackson said, creeping closer to Edgar, smiling eerily.

"SHUT UP!" Edgar screamed, pulling at his long hair and nearly tearing out a chunk of it.

Jackson disappeared.

"Edgar, who are you telling to shut up?" Barbara asked, looking first at Liam, then around the kitchen.

Edgar shoved Liam away and smiled warmly. "Don't worry, Mom. Nothing's going on. We're just friends."

"Are you sure you're okay, Edgar?" Barbara asked.

"I'm fine," Edgar said calmly, shrugging his shoulders.

Barbara worriedly looked at Edgar, while Edgar glanced at Liam and saw his pained expression before he composed himself.

"The tacos should be ready soon," Liam said, clearing his throat and avoiding eye contact with Edgar, as he pulled out plates from the cupboard.

"Well…I'm glad you have a new friend," Barbara said.

Edgar still reeled from his latest encounter with Jackson. Was it really him? Was it Jackson's ghost coming back to haunt him? Or a manifestation of his deepest fears? The same questions rotated through Edgar's mind and he didn't feel any closer to answering them. He thought going to Minnesota, returning to his childhood home, and spending time with his parents would help. But what if they were part of the reason his memories wouldn't come back? Edgar wondered if there was more to the story his mom told about his dad kicking him out and disowning him from the family. He could have suffered severe trauma and his subconscious could be repressing the memories because they were too painful. Maybe it was better if he didn't remember.

# Chapter 18: Delia

Natalia passed away peacefully during the night. Delia slept at her apartment; it didn't make sense for her to sleep in an uncomfortable chair at the hospital when she lived close by. Besides, her mom didn't recognize her anymore, and threw a fit half the time when someone was in her room.

Delia rushed to the hospital when Dr. Rutger called. Although she realized it didn't matter how quickly she reached the hospital, it still seemed important for her to be there as soon as possible. When she arrived, Dr. Rutger left her alone with her mom for a few minutes so she could say goodbye.

Delia always found it strange when people kissed their dead loved one or stroked their hand or held them one last time. She knew her mom's soul was no longer in her body and there was no point in giving it any affection, so she simply whispered, "I love you, Mom. I'm sorry I wasn't there for you in your final moments," and left the room.

Although Delia thought about what would happen next, she hadn't planned on it happening so quickly. She assumed, wrongfully apparently, that she had weeks, maybe even months, until her mom would be gone. One of the only positives to come out of her mom's passing was that now Delia could finally allow herself to plan the trip to Minneapolis without feeling remorse. The worst already happened. Her mom was dead, but now wasn't the time to mourn and let herself fall to pieces. She had a serial killer to apprehend.

***

Delia quickly made funeral arrangements and planned the funeral for the following weekend. Jerry, Becca and Joel, and her former boss, Will, each made an appearance. Even if she didn't have many people in her life, she was thankful for the ones who were there for her. Delia began packing for Minneapolis to keep her mind off of her mom's death. Distractions were good right now. As she folded clothes and tried to decide which outfits to bring on her trip, her phone rang.

"Hello?" Delia said.

"Hey, what are you up to right now?" Becca asked.

"Packing for Minneapolis. I might do some cleaning tonight too."

"Okay, good. I'm on my way over. I'll be there in about ten minutes," Becca responded.

Delia sighed exasperatedly. "You don't need to come over, Becca. I'm fine."

"No, you're not. I've known you since we were teenagers. I know you don't want to be by yourself while you're dealing with…everything."

"Fine. I can't promise I'll be good company though," Delia said.

"Don't worry; I'm coming over to hang out and make sure you're not alone on such a terrible night. I'll see you soon," Becca said, ending the phone call.

Delia gave up on packing and left her suitcase and bedroom in disarray to enter the family room. She browsed her DVD collection, wondering what she and Becca should watch while they hung out. Delia didn't know what type of movie she was in the mood for, definitely nothing too cheesy or happy. She pulled out a few DVDs from the entertainment center and threw them on the coffee table. Delia sat on the couch, mindlessly scrolling through social media on her phone, waiting for Becca to arrive.

The doorbell rang what felt like an eternity later to Delia and she answered the door with a forced smile.

Becca greeted her with a hug. She wore fleece sweatpants and a heavy sweater much too big on her that probably belonged to Joel. "How are you doing, Delia?" She asked sympathetically, entering the apartment and setting the plastic bag she held on the counter.

"I'm okay," Delia said, following Becca into the kitchen and smiling even bigger.

Becca raised an eyebrow. "Your smile is so fake. Luckily, I brought a few things to ensure this is a fun night for both of us."

Becca opened the plastic bag and pulled out a half gallon tub of chocolate brownie ice cream, a bag of M&M's, potato chips, and a bottle of wine.

"Have I mentioned lately how much I love you?" Delia said, grabbing the tub of ice cream and immediately popping off the lid.

"You might have mentioned it once or twice."

"I wasn't sure what we should watch while we hang out, but I pulled out a few DVDs from my collection," Delia said, scooping generous portions of ice cream into two bowls, then pouring M&M's on top.

Becca smiled and grabbed a bowl, making herself comfortable on the couch. "Did you ever wonder if we would stop eating junk food when we got older? Because I definitely thought I would eat healthier when I became an adult."

Delia snorted and took a giant bite of her ice cream. "Nope. When I was a kid, I hoped I would eat ice cream whenever I wanted as an adult. And that came true, so I guess younger me would be proud of adult me."

"Geez, Delia, what's with all the movies you picked? *Halloween, Texas Chainsaw Massacre, A Nightmare on Elm Street, Psycho...*" Becca said, naming the movies as she flipped through the DVDs and tossed them aside one by one.

"Sorry, I'm not in the mood to watch an upbeat and positive movie. Besides, I can't shake the Jackson Birkman case from my mind," Delia said, pausing as she realized that was how everyone referred to the case, even though Jackson's fiancée, Clara, had also been murdered. How sad was that to be reduced to nothing more than a celebrity's fiancée?

Becca licked ice cream off the spoon and scooped another spoonful from her bowl. "You're not going to let it go, are you?"

"No. I tried, but I can't."

"It's not your fault—" Becca started to say, but Delia interrupted.

"Of course you're going to say that. Everyone has told me a hundred times. It doesn't matter. I feel responsible for whatever happens while Edgar is still free to roam the world and do as he pleases."

"You can't blame yourself for what he does. If he's the one who killed Jackson and Clara and tried to make it seem like a murder-suicide by Clara's hand, then he's a psychopath," Becca said emphatically.

Delia nodded. "I know, but I'm the only one who thinks Edgar is guilty, so I'm the only one who can stop him. It has to be me."

"I thought you stopped being a police officer to avoid these types of situations—you know, putting yourself in danger?" Becca questioned.

Delia continued eating her ice cream in silence for several scoops before answering. "I did. I thought I made the right choice at the time, but the more I thought about it and the more time that passed, I realized I need to stop him."

Becca hesitated before speaking. "Well, what if Edgar hasn't killed anyone since then? What if he's trying to live a normal life and hasn't hurt anyone?"

Delia violently shook her head. "No. People like that don't just stop killing. They might slow down or take a temporary break, but they always become restless and kill again. I know he's going to if he hasn't already."

"Okay. You're the expert," Becca said, hands raised in frustration.

"You don't believe me?" Delia asked, surprised.

"No. I mean, I understand that you know a lot more about criminals and murderers than me. That's one of the reasons why you're always one of my beta readers for my books. Your experience and knowledge from being a police officer gives great insight into criminals' minds. But, since the Birkman case wasn't resolved how you wanted it to be, I wonder if your obsession is futile. I don't want to discourage you if you aren't going to give up on it, but I also don't want it to ruin your mental health if you aren't able to capture Edgar a second time. How are you planning on arresting him? Do you have recent charges you can bring against him?"

Delia ran her hands through her curly red hair. It was tangled and badly needed to be washed. "You're right, Becca. I don't have any charges I can arrest him for," Delia admitted, feeling more lost and hopeless than ever.

"I'm sure you'll figure it out. Don't you have that private detective helping you?"

"Yeah, maybe he has an idea," Delia said hopefully, scooping up the last bite of her ice cream. "I think I'm ready for those chips."

Becca stayed the night with Delia because she didn't want to leave her alone. They slept together in Delia's bed, just like when they were teenagers. Delia slept peacefully for the first time in months.

# Chapter 19: Edgar

Edgar slept in his childhood bedroom. It had been converted into a guest bedroom/office/workout room because it was the only spare bedroom in the small house. He rested on the queen-sized bed with flannel sheets and a heavy quilt covering him, but despite feeling quite cozy and exhausted from the events that transpired earlier in the day, he still struggled to fall asleep at 2:00 a.m. Liam slept on the couch in the living room. Edgar kept thinking about what his mom said. About how his parents kicked him out, how his mom didn't resist when his dad disowned him, how they were disappointed with their gay son. As if being gay was a choice he made. The only solace Edgar felt was knowing that his dad would be dead soon. Although his mom didn't say much about the situation, it didn't sound as if he would be around much longer. Edgar wanted to see his dad one more time, if only to show off Liam and see his reaction.

*Thud. Thud. Thud.* Edgar sat up in bed, wondering where the noise came from. He assumed the house had a basement, but his mom hadn't offered to give them a tour of the house. Thinking back, Edgar wondered, was that strange? Earlier, Barbara ran into the hallway to block Edgar's path when he tried walking toward the bedrooms. Something was going on and he was determined to figure it out. He hopped out of bed and grabbed a t-shirt and jeans, quickly dressed, and used his cellphone's flashlight to light his path out of the room and into the hallway.

"Shoot" he heard coming from what sounded like the basement. Was his mom down there? What was she doing this late at night? Although she didn't seem fragile, she wasn't exactly young anymore and she was overweight, so if she tripped and fell down the stairs, she could be hurt.

"Mom?" Edgar called, creeping to the door where he was pretty sure the noise came from.

He turned the doorknob and slowly walked down the stairs, nearly every stair creaking as he descended into the basement. "Mom?" Edgar called again, hoping she would answer.

Even if he wasn't happy with his parents for how they treated him, that didn't mean he wanted them to be hurt. Or at least, not his mom.

"Oh, darn," Barbara said as she watched Edgar descend the last stair and walk into the basement, finding Barbara dragging a large man's body across the floor.

"What the hell?" Edgar exclaimed, backing up towards the stairs again. "What are you doing?!"

Barbara dropped the man's body with another loud *thud* and leaned against the wall, wiping the sweat from her brow. "Shh, be quiet, Edgar!" His mom shushed him. "I planned to dispose of him today, but then you and Liam showed up, so my plans were delayed. I waited until I thought you were both asleep, but he's so heavy it was a struggle to stay quiet."

Edgar inspected the dead man. He was tall and overweight, with only a few wisps of gray hair on his round head. His skin looked ghastly white and Edgar wondered if it was a side effect of the cancer or from chemo. Or did his mom lie to him about his dad having cancer too? How did he know he could trust anything she told him?

"Is that Dad?" Edgar asked quietly, staring at the man's body sprawled out on the cool concrete floor.

Barbara's chest heaved as she struggled to catch her breath. "Yes, it is—*was* your dad."

"Um, okay. What happened to him?" Edgar didn't feel frightened. He mostly wondered why his mom dragged his dad's body down the basement stairs and what she planned on doing with it.

"I told you. He was diagnosed with lung cancer and he—he couldn't fight it anymore," Barbara said, putting her hand over her mouth and slumping onto a chair pushed against the wall.

"I thought you said he was in the hospital? And that I could go visit him. It doesn't look like I'll be able to talk to him now," Edgar said, holding back the laughter that threatened to erupt.

"He was in the hospital for months, Edgar. I brought him home because I didn't want him to die there surrounded by strangers and no one who loves him," Barbara said.

"I can't tell if you're lying about the cancer, but I don't think that's what killed him," Edgar said, circling his dad's body, looking for wounds, a gunshot, bruises, or any other sign of harm. "How did you do it?" He asked curiously, looking up at his mom from his crouched position on the concrete, hovering over his dead dad.

"Do what?" Barbara asked, placing her hands on her knees and still struggling to steady her breathing.

Edgar shook his long hair out of his eyes and picked up his dad's arm, looking at it closely. "If he *did* have cancer and was weakened from undergoing chemo treatment, I suppose you could have overpowered him. Did you suffocate him? Or poison him? If you were taking care of him, it would have been so simple to slip poison into his food without him noticing."

"Edgar," Barbara gasped, shocked and still out of breath. "How dare you suggest I would do something so terrible? I know you're claiming to have lost your memory, but if you knew a thing about me, you would know how much I loved your dad."

"I'm sure you did love him. At one point. But, if you told the truth earlier about Dad kicking me out and essentially banishing me while you harbored guilt and resentment for the past ten years, then I can understand how that would lead you to this," Edgar said logically, as if he spoke about scientific facts.

Barbara quickly shook her head back and forth. "No, you're wrong. I didn't hurt him. He died from lung cancer."

Edgar paused before asking, "When did he die?"

"A few days ago," Barbara responded, chewing on her nails.

A sinister smile crept across Edgar's face and his already dark eyes seemed to darken even more in the dim light of the basement. A creaking sound came from upstairs.

"Oh, Edgar! You're being too loud. You must have woken up Liam," Barbara said, shushing him, even though he hadn't been talking.

"Don't worry, Mom. I won't say a word. If Liam tries to come down here, tell him you were rearranging some furniture because you couldn't sleep, but you're going to bed soon so there's no need for him to come down."

Barbara nodded, not wanting to say another word out loud until they were certain Liam wasn't coming downstairs. Edgar and Barbara waited in silence for a few minutes but the house was completely silent.

"Maybe he got up to use the restroom," Barbara said quietly.

"What were you planning on doing with the body after you brought it down here?" Edgar whispered.

"I'm not sure. I didn't think that far ahead," Barbara said, stumbling over her words.

"Yes, you did. You don't seem dumb to me. I don't think you would have followed through with it without a plan, so tell me. I'll help you."

"There's a lake nearby," Barbara responded quickly, keeping her voice lowered. "If you take the path through the woods in our backyard, it leads to a manmade lake. It's still partially frozen over because it's so cold and it won't fully thaw for at least a few more months. Sometimes it even takes until the summer to fully thaw. I planned to dump his body in the lake."

Edgar stroked the stubble on his chin thoughtfully. "I think we can do better. We need to make sure that when the lake thaws and someone finds the body, it's unrecognizable."

Barbara nodded slowly. "I have some sulfuric acid in the garage. We could use that and then throw the body in the lake."

Edgar giggled and put his hand over his mouth in surprise.

"What? Why are you laughing, Edgar? This isn't funny. I'll go to prison if anyone finds out what happened," Barbara said sternly.

Edgar rolled his eyes. "Mom, I didn't even question why you have sulfuric acid in your garage. No one randomly has powerful acids lying around. The murder was premeditated. Admit you killed him. I'm not going to judge you."

Barbara eyed him wearily. "Did you…do something bad too?"

Edgar thought about the mechanic whose head he smashed in with the wrench. The gouge in his head. The blood that pooled on the floor by the body. The power that surged through him as he stood over the mechanic, draining his life force away. "That's not important. We have a body to discard!" Edgar said cheerily.

Barbara sighed and looked at her husband's body. "Why are you so darn cheerful, Edgar? That's your dad lying there. I know you don't remember him, but he was a good man. He tried his best to be a decent father and husband, but we were raised in different times. Marriages were seen differently back then and parenting styles were too."

Edgar spit on his dad's body. "Stop trying to defend him. If he wasn't okay with me being gay, then he doesn't even deserve a funeral. No one should mourn him or celebrate his life. He wasn't worth it."

"Oh, Edgar. I know it's hard for you to forgive, but please try to let it go. Let the past stay in the past and move on."

Edgar laughed harshly. "Mom, you clearly didn't 'let it go.' Don't lecture me about forgiveness."

Barbara rushed to Edgar's side and wrapped her arms around his thin body. "I love you. I forgive you for everything you did. I understand why you acted that way. Do you forgive me?"

Edgar squeezed his mom tightly and for a minute wondered if he should squeeze harder and harder until her breathing became ragged and then she couldn't breathe at all. He let go of her and relaxed his tense muscles. "Forgive me for what? What did I do?"

Barbara frowned. "You never had any friends until you met Jackson. Since you stayed friends with him over the years, I thought you would become popular and have lots of friends and a girlfriend. I thought you would find someone and fall in love, get married, and have a kid or two someday, but you never found any of that," Barbara paused, clearing her throat. "The first time it happened, you were only three. I still don't know where you found it. Maybe in the woods somewhere? You were playing in the backyard. You always loved to be outside and I encouraged it because it made you happy. You came running up to me. I was in the front yard tending the garden. You were holding a dead cat and a huge rock. The cat was battered and bloody and your matching Gymboree t-shirt and pants were covered in blood. At first, I couldn't believe it. I grabbed the cat and the rock from you and buried it in the woods. I told you to keep it a secret because I didn't know what you were thinking or why you did it. You were only three…"

Edgar pursed his lips. "I killed a cat? I think I remember killing another one. Last year. Jackson's fiancée had a cat. I think I killed her cat too," he said, reflecting on what this meant.

Barbara sobbed quietly, tears running down her wrinkled face. "I tried to protect you. As your mother, I knew it was my duty to protect you. I didn't want you to keep doing it, but you wouldn't stop. No matter what I did or threatened you with, you always killed again. It was like a compulsion for you. I never told your dad, but I think he knew. Or at least suspected something was wrong. We had so many arguments where he tried to convince me we should send you away because something was 'off' about you. I always told him I would never give up on you. I would never cast you out of the house or out of the family because you're my son. I always protected you, Edgar."

Edgar contemplated his mom's words, wondering if she told the truth. Why did he doubt everyone so much? Since his dad was dead now, he could never ask him what happened or hear his side of the story. It was difficult to piece everything together, especially when he still didn't have all his memories back and couldn't be certain that his mom lied. "So, after the first cat, when did it happen again?" He finally asked. Even if she was telling a story, he wanted to know how she perceived his childhood.

"I didn't want to bring this up. It's difficult for me to talk about. I think it's for the best that you don't know the worst thing you did," Barbara said.

"Please tell me. I need to know who I was."

"Fine, but even though you did all those terrible things it doesn't mean you have to be that person anymore. You have a chance to start over. To be better."

Edgar grinned with a dark glint in his eyes. "Don't worry. I'll do it right this time."

Barbara inhaled deeply, held her breath for a few seconds, and then exhaled loudly. "A few months after the cat, I found you playing with a dead turtle. You said you found it in front of the house, near the street, but I kept thinking about the cat and wondered if you were old enough to know how to lie convincingly. Afterwards, every few months I would find a dead animal in the garage or in the backyard. You were too young to know how to discard it. I think you learned pretty quickly that I would clean up your mess, so your dad would never find out." Barbara stopped talking, whether she was thinking about how to proceed or pondering her young son's descent into madness was unclear.

"Is that it?" Edgar asked, tilting his head to the side.

"No," Barbara grimaced. "I wish. Later in the year, I got pregnant again. Your dad didn't want another kid because he thought you were enough of a handful. He tried to make me have an abortion, but I always wanted more kids, so I followed through with the pregnancy. Your brother was born when you were four. We named him Eliot, after T.S. Eliot. When he was born, you were jealous. You didn't like that I wasn't doting on you every minute of every day and I didn't have enough time to clean up your messes. You probably felt neglected." Barbara's breathing became louder as she struggled to continue speaking. "One day, you were with Eliot in the bedroom you shared. We put his crib in your bedroom since we didn't have another room for him to sleep in. Your dad was outside mowing the lawn and I was in the kitchen cooking dinner. He was laying in his crib and crying. I knew you were in the room with him, so I thought you would try to quiet him down, maybe play with him."

Barbara stopped talking, gathering herself before she could continue again. Edgar leaned forward eagerly in anticipation of what was coming next.

Barbara took a deep breath before speaking. "His crying stopped a few minutes later, then it was completely silent for what seemed like too long, so I went into your bedroom to make sure you and Eliot were both okay. When you have two small children, silence is always suspicious. I went in your bedroom and you were sitting on the area rug and holding Eliot in your arms. At first, I thought he was okay. You were smiling so big and rocking him. I remember telling you that you were being such a good big brother and thanking you for helping me take care of him. Then, when I went to take him from your arms, I realized he was too still. He wasn't breathing. I tried to give him CPR and screamed at you to call 911. You never admitted to anything and when the police asked what happened, we guessed that Eliot died from SIDS because he was sleeping in his crib. And for all I know, that could have been what happened. You were only four. You were so young. Maybe you didn't know he was dead when you picked him up. You must not have known. Otherwise, if he was still alive when you took him out of the crib…" Barbara trailed off, shuddering, unable to finish the sentence. "No, Eliot died from SIDS. That's what we told the police and that's what happened. There's no other possible explanation."

Edgar enjoyed hearing his mom talk about his childhood. He wondered what else he did that he couldn't remember. How many animals did he kill? Did he ever try to murder someone, besides Eliot, if that was what really happened? Did it matter now since he was in his thirties and all of those things happened so long ago? And most importantly, did knowing about his fascination with death and killing from such a young age make him more certain that he was heading down the same path?

"Well, we need to get rid of this body tonight," Barbara said, abruptly changing the subject and glancing at the Fitbit on her wrist. "It's after 3:00 a.m. now! Will you help me carry him to the lake?"

"First, we need to dissolve as much of the body as possible. You said you had some sulfuric acid in the garage? The body won't be identifiable and they won't be able to trace it back to us," Edgar said.

"You were always such a smart boy. Will sulfuric acid be powerful enough? The laundry room is down here and there's a pretty big sink in there. We could fill it with the chemicals and put the body in there to dissolve it," Barbara said.

"Is the sink big enough to fit the body?" Edgar wondered. "What if we cut him up first?"

Barbara gasped. "Edgar, how dare you suggest doing that to your dad! He may be dead, but he's still your dad."

"You're the one who killed him, Mom. I'm trying to help you dispose of the body and all the evidence."

Barbara's eyes filled with tears and she hastily brushed them away when they started to run down her cheeks. "Please help me, Edgar," she sobbed, grabbing his hands. "I do want your help. I'm not strong enough to do this by myself."

"I will help you. Listen to me. Do you have a saw?"

Barbara's face whitened. "Yes, I'll go find it and the chemicals."

Edgar nodded. "Okay and I'll bring the body into the laundry room."

Edgar lifted his dad's body by himself and clumsily half-carried, half-dragged it into the nearby laundry room, a small room off of the main part of the basement. The light flickered as he flipped the switch to assess the laundry room and the sink faucet dripped a steady rhythm. He let go of his dad's body and set it against the laundry room sink, breathing heavily from the exertion.

Barbara returned a few minutes later with a saw and the sulfuric acid they hoped would dissolve the body. Or most of it.

"Here, this is it," Barbara said, setting down the supplies.

Edgar put the stopper in the sink and picked up the jug of chemicals, dumping all of it into the sink. He picked up the saw and looked at his dad's ashen face as he bent over him, preparing to make the first cut. "Bye, Dad. I don't remember you, but you sounded like a dick, so I don't feel too bad about doing this to you."

Edgar stood with the saw poised over his dad's body, ready to slice through his left arm, when his mom grabbed his arm to stop him.

"Edgar!" Barbara exclaimed. "I can't watch. I know I—it's my fault, but I can't watch this."

"Okay, go wait in the main part of the basement then. This won't take long," Edgar said, as his mom ran out of the laundry room and hastily closed the door.

Edgar grinned as he placed the saw against his dad's cool flesh and began to cut, moving the saw back and forth, slicing through the flesh, and trying to cut through the bone. He wiped blood and sweat from his forehead as he continuously hacked away at his dad's arms, legs, and head. He thought it would be easier to dissolve if there were smaller pieces.

Edgar wasn't sure how harmful sulfuric acid was and didn't want to find out what would happen if he accidentally let it touch his skin. He pulled a pair of rubber gloves onto his hands after finding them in a cabinet in the laundry room. He picked up one of his dad's sawn-off arms and carefully placed it in the laundry room sink, which was full nearly to the brim with the clear, viscous liquid. He hoped their plan would work. He used the end of a broom to push the arm underneath the liquid and watched as it began to slowly dissolve. He realized he didn't know how long it would take or if the chemicals would be capable of dissolving bones and teeth. Was it worrisome that he couldn't stop smiling as he looked at the laundry room sink full of hacked off body parts? It's not like he killed him. He didn't do anything wrong this time. He was only trying to help his mom.

# Chapter 20: Delia

Becca left early to meet Joel for breakfast, leaving Delia alone. Delia didn't mind. She appreciated Becca coming over and staying the night with her, but she also thought having some time for herself would let her sort through her feelings and ponder her next move. Delia flipped through the Jackson Birkman case file once again. As she shut the manila folder, a photo slid out and onto the floor. She carefully picked it up, unsure what it was. When she looked at it, she remembered the day she saw Edgar on the news with a mysterious man. The printed photo was the one shown on every news channel since Edgar was spotted. Delia knew she needed to figure out who the man was with Edgar.

Delia called Jerry, assuming he could help. His years of experience as a private detective meant he had connections in all sorts of useful places.

"Hey, Jerry," she said when he answered the phone.

"What's up? How are you?" Jerry asked kindly.

"I've been better. I was looking at my research and notes for the Jackson Birkman case. I keep coming back to the photo of Edgar with the mystery man that was shown on the news. I think the man he was with in Mexico must have some significance. Can we find out who he is before we go to Minneapolis?"

"Good idea, it's worth a shot. I'll call a buddy of mine who's a detective in Mexico and see if he can match the photo to anyone living near Lake Chapala," Jerry said, enthusiastically.

"Oh, that would be great, Jerry! Thank you. I think we're onto something. What if this man is also a criminal? We could have him arrested and wait for Edgar to show up and then apprehend him."

"We don't know for sure that they're connected. There's a chance he happened to be captured in the photo with Edgar, and Edgar doesn't actually know him."

"You're right. It's a long shot, but I'm holding out hope that we will solve this case. This could be a piece of the puzzle we need," Delia said.

"I admire your optimism, Delia," Jerry replied, laughing. "I'll let you know after I hear back from my connection."

After her phone call with Jerry, Delia continued perusing the Jackson Birkman case file. She still thought she was overlooking a key element, but hoped investigating the man Edgar was seen with would shed some light. She kept revisiting the conversations she had with Edgar when she interrogated him, first as a close friend of both Jackson and Clara, then as a potential suspect. She wondered if anything Edgar said during their conversations was revealing. Delia knew from her memories and the copious notes she took that Edgar loaned great sums of money to Jackson for quite some time. Even though Edgar brushed it off as simply helping out a friend, Delia knew there had been more to it. Not even the best friend in the world would loan their friend hundreds of thousands of dollars without expecting a favor in return. The question was, what had Edgar expected? What did he want from Jackson? And why had he killed him?

Delia tapped her pen against her pages of notes and idly turned the pages, feeling as if she was on the verge of a great discovery. She flipped over a handwritten page torn out of one of her notebooks and looked at the back of the page, on which she could barely read what she wrote: *Did Edgar have feelings for Jackson?* Apparently after she wrote it down, she thought the idea was crazy and lazily crossed it out. But now, after forcing herself to spend months away from the case and not constantly looking at her notes, despite her obsession, Delia wondered again if Edgar had feelings for Jackson. At the time of his death, Jackson was newly engaged to Clara. He was going to marry the supposed love of his life after finally committing to her. If Edgar had feelings for Jackson, the idea of Jackson marrying Clara could have made him crazy, especially if Edgar was the only one who knew about Jackson's financial trouble and was the one Jackson turned to any time he needed help.

Delia set down the piece of notebook paper and brushed her hair back from her face. She had reflected on every possible theory for months, but her latest idea made the most sense. If it had been a crime of passion, that gave Edgar the ultimate motive.

After a few hours, Delia decided to take a break from browsing her notes and case files to eat lunch. She still needed to finish packing for Minneapolis but couldn't find the motivation to continue being productive until she knew if the mystery man in the photo with Edgar was connected to him.

She decided to sauté a few pieces of chicken and onions in a skillet on the stovetop and watch Netflix while she ate lunch. Delia wondered if it was depressing that she couldn't eat a meal alone without watching TV or listening to a podcast. There was something to be said about people and their obsession with constant stimulation. No one could enjoy a meal in silence or sit and think without something else going on in the background to distract them from their reality.

As Delia finished her lunch and cleaned up the kitchen, her phone rang.

"Hello?" She answered excitedly. It was Jerry. She hoped he had information about Edgar's mysterious friend.

"Hey, Delia. I didn't think I would have an answer for you this quickly, but my buddy in Mexico was interested in helping out when I explained the case and the possible connection between Edgar and the man in the photo."

"Yeah?" Delia said impatiently.

Jerry chuckled. "So, after having one of his guys run the photo through their software, they found a match. His name is Liam Black. He's from Asheville, North Carolina and he's an American citizen. Apparently, he moved to Lake Chapala a few years ago. But, here's the crazy part. He had a sister and parents who lived in Asheville also, but they all died in a house fire a few years ago, before Liam moved to Lake Chapala."

Delia gasped. "Was Liam involved in the fire?" She asked immediately, her mind racing.

"The police questioned Liam after the fire, but he wasn't home when it happened. He worked as a seasonal sales associate in retail and his boss vouched for him. They had no reason to believe it was his fault. In fact, after the home was inspected, they closed the case and deemed the cause of the fire was the result of bad wiring, an electrical issue common in older homes that aren't up to code," Jerry said.

"Was your friend able to provide any insight about whether Liam and Edgar know each other?"

"No, but it does seem more likely there is a connection after finding out about Liam's entire family dying in a fire while he conveniently wasn't home. I'm not sure how Liam and Edgar met, but if they knew each other before Edgar went to Lake Chapala, it's possible they've been working together the entire time."

Delia quickly scribbled a few notes about the information Jerry told her. "Thank you, Jerry. I really appreciate your help, especially pulling in one of your connections on this case. I never would have figured out who Liam was on my own. At least not this quickly."

"No problem. Do you think we'll be heading to Minneapolis soon? I'm anxious to travel there now. What do you think the chances are that two murderers would team up together?" Jerry pondered.

"I never considered it, but I'm sure it doesn't happen often," Delia responded wryly, browsing Google flights on her phone to see when the next flight from New York City to Minneapolis departed. "And the next flight from JFK to Minneapolis leaves tomorrow morning at 5:00 a.m. Is that okay? I'll buy the plane tickets right now."

"Sounds good. I'll swing by your apartment in the morning to pick you up, so we don't have to leave both of our cars at the airport while we're out of town. Airports always charge an astronomical fee for long-term parking."

"Thanks again, Jerry. See you tomorrow morning," Delia said, ending the phone call and eagerly perusing her new notes.

She quickly added to what she already wrote in her notebook and felt as if she could finally breathe for the first time in months. Delia finished packing in a rush and decided to go on a run. She had been a runner in high school and wasn't sure what prompted her to want to exercise suddenly, but she followed her intuition, knowing the exercise and fresh air would be good for her.

As her feet pounded on the pavement, she became excited about her trip to Minneapolis with Jerry. Although they had planned the trip for what seemed like forever, since they already canceled it once, it didn't feel like it was happening this time. After her run, Delia decided to stop at the donut shop near her apartment. She deserved a treat. Ever since Jackson was kidnapped, Delia couldn't fully rest. Her mind constantly churned out new theories and hypothesized where Edgar was and what he was doing. She hoped the case would be resolved once and for all after she confronted Edgar. She assumed he would be caught off guard. He probably thought he was safe. If Edgar was staying at his parent's house, her mission was nearly complete. She didn't consider what would happen if Edgar *wasn't* in Minneapolis. She had a strong suspicion he was hiding in Minneapolis and didn't want to waste her time pondering other possibilities until she knew for sure. Delia didn't think he would go down easily, but if he confessed to the murders or revealed his true nature, it would make it a lot easier to detain him and bring him back to New York, since that was where the murders occurred.

Delia ate the donuts gleefully and laid out her clothes for the next morning. She knew her life wouldn't be better immediately, but she finally felt hopeful about the future. Around 10:00 p.m., she decided she should try to sleep, so she wouldn't be exhausted when they arrived in Minneapolis the next day. She tossed and turned as a dozen questions about Edgar, Liam, and Jackson ran through her mind. Eventually, she fell into a restless sleep.

When Delia's alarm went off at 3:00 a.m., she groaned, knowing she needed to get out of bed, gather her belongings for the trip, and be ready to leave when Jerry arrived. She slowly dressed and brushed her hair, deciding unnecessary tasks such as showering and putting on makeup were only meant for people who didn't wake up this early.

Jerry arrived a half hour later and helped Delia load her bags into the trunk of his car. When they arrived at the airport, after checking in with their flight and going through security, they beelined for the Starbucks. Jerry ordered a venti black coffee, while Delia ordered a grande café mocha. It was the closest she ever came to enjoying coffee. Shortly after, they boarded the flight. As the plane took off from the ground, Delia stared out the window, watching the ascent into the sky, silently saying her final goodbyes to her beloved city in case she didn't make it home. Her stomach flipped as the plane sped up, anxiety threatening to overcome her.

Jerry noticed Delia's silent apprehension and tightly wound fingers clutching the armrest. He distracted her by discussing the sights he wanted to see while they were in Minneapolis. Delia was glad she wasn't making the trip alone.

# Chapter 21: Edgar

Edgar helped his mom carry a bucket containing the pieces of his dad that didn't dissolve to the lake, so they could dump them in the water and hope no one ever found out what they did. Barbara would tell everyone her husband died from his long battle with lung cancer and no one would be surprised because he smoked a pack a day for over forty years. When they reached the lake, Edgar peered into the bucket one last time. His dad's deformed head was in there, half-dissolved, as well as his teeth, which Edgar had carefully chipped out of the mouth, and most of his bones that hadn't fully dissolved in the chemicals.

Edgar pulled out the hammer he brought on their twisted excursion and knelt beside the frozen, manmade lake. He tapped the frozen surface with the hammer several times, watching tiny cracks appear and expand, spider-webbing across the lake. After a final tap, Edgar stepped off the lake, not wanting to accidentally fall in through the ice. He leapt to safety right as the cracks spread and split open, revealing the flowing water below the surface. He tossed the bucket of bones, teeth, and body parts into the water and watched them become carried away by the current, mixing in with the chunks of ice. Barbara sobbed next to him, leaning on his shoulder for support.

"It's okay, Mom," Edgar said, comfortingly patting her on the back. "Everything will be okay."

After their late-night adventure, Edgar and Barbara returned to the house and went to sleep. Edgar slept through the night without waking up again.

When Edgar woke later in the morning, the scent of bacon and eggs wafted into the spare bedroom. He wandered into the kitchen and found Barbara and Liam sitting at the table, enjoying breakfast and coffee. He smiled, feeling a twinge of happiness at the sight of his newfound family members getting along.

"Good morning, Edgar," Barbara greeted him as he sat in the chair next to Liam.

"Morning, Edgar," Liam said.

"Morning," Edgar replied, still half-asleep but invigorated from the previous night's events.

Barbara set a plate of bacon and eggs in front of him. "Coffee?" She asked with a small smile, holding the coffee pot, and placing a mug by Edgar's plate.

"Of course," Edgar responded, holding the coffee mug while Barbara poured coffee into it. "Thanks, Mom."

Barbara's smile waned, but she attempted to put it back in place and returned to her seat at the worn kitchen table. "What do you two have planned for today?"

Liam turned to Edgar earnestly, pushing his empty plate aside. "We could explore the city. I've never been to Minneapolis before and since you don't remember living here, I think it would be fun to walk around downtown. I looked up things to do in the area. We could see a play at The Guthrie Theater or go hiking at Minnehaha Falls. There are also a bunch of coffee shops and breweries nearby that sound great. What do you think?"

"Sure, yeah. We can do whatever," Edgar said noncommittally, tearing off a chunk of bacon with his teeth.

"Oh. Okay. I thought we should take advantage of our time in Minneapolis," Liam responded, crestfallen.

"You're right," Edgar finally said. "Let's go to Minnehaha Falls."

"I'll pack some snacks for you two. You could easily spend an entire day hiking and enjoying the beautiful waterfalls," Barbara said.

"You aren't coming with us?" Edgar asked.

"No. I have a few…chores to take care of around the house," Barbara said, shooting a meaningful look at Edgar.

"Right. Of course. Is it okay if we take your car then if you don't need it for the next few hours?" Edgar said.

"Sure," Barbara responded as she packed up granola bars, crackers, and water bottles for Edgar and Liam to bring on their hike. "The keys are on the counter," she said, vaguely pointing.

"We'll only be gone a few hours," Liam told Barbara. "We can pick up lunch too."

When Edgar and Liam arrived at Minnehaha Falls, Edgar was taken aback by the breathtaking waterfalls. Since it was early April in Minnesota, there weren't many people at the falls. It was a rare spring day with no snow on the ground, warm enough that most of the water wasn't frozen over. But the air was still frigid and whipped ferociously at Edgar and Liam as they entered the park and headed towards one of the trails.

After they walked for a while, Liam broke the silence. "What were you and Barbara doing last night?" He asked quietly, even though no one was on the trail with them.

"What are you talking about?" Edgar said, feigning innocence.

"Come on, Edgar. You don't have to lie to me. I saw you kill the mechanic. I know what type of person you are."

"You do? Then why do you still want to be with me?"

Liam's breathing became ragged as they continued their ascent up a particularly steep part of the trail. "Can we stop for a minute? I think I'm going to pass out."

Edgar was slightly ahead of Liam on the trail, so he turned around to join Liam just off the path. He handed him the bag with the snacks and water bottles.

Liam shook his head and grabbed Edgar's hands, gently holding them in his own hands, but Edgar immediately pulled his hands away.

"What are you doing?" Edgar asked Liam.

"I'm sorry if I tried to be a little romantic while telling you I love you for the first time!" Liam yelled, throwing up his hands in frustration.

Edgar groaned. He sat down on a large boulder and put his head in his hands and finally made eye contact with Liam after a moment of silence. "Look, Liam, I don't want to hurt you, but…"

Liam interrupted him. "No, I know what you're going to say, but it's not true. I know you love me too."

"I don't though. You were the first person I met in Mexico and you helped me so much when I didn't have any money or a job or a place to stay. It would have been rude if I told you to leave me alone. And I *do* appreciate all your help. I just don't feel the same way."

"You don't mean that."

Edgar sighed and swept his long, dark hair back from his face. "I didn't think it would go on for this long. Honestly, I didn't think you would stay with me after I killed the mechanic." Edgar shook his head in wonder. "Since it doesn't matter now, I might as well tell you. My mom killed my dad the day before we arrived, so yesterday I helped her dissolve his body and we threw the pieces that wouldn't dissolve into the lake, in the woods behind their house. His head only partially dissolved and the teeth and bones were difficult as well—"

Liam cut him off again, his face turning a sickly shade of white. "Edgar, what are you saying?" He paced across the side of the trail, creating more distance between himself and Edgar.

"I thought it was pretty clear. My mom killed my dad and I helped her dispose of the body and the evidence. He sounded like an asshole."

"Why didn't you wake me up and tell me what was going on last night? Or better yet, turn her in to the police?"

Edgar rolled his eyes. "She's my mom, Liam. I'm not going to betray her. She's the only family I have left now. Besides, she told me about my childhood and how she protected me for years."

"What did she protect you from?" Liam asked.

"Oh, well I always brought home dead animals as a kid and cut them open, trying to figure out how their insides looked. Sometimes I even kept the bones. Apparently, I've been fascinated with death since a young age," Edgar said, grinning.

Liam's face whitened even more. "I never told you what happened in Asheville that made me move to Mexico. It might help you understand me more and why I think we're meant to be together."

"Yeah?"

"You have to understand how horribly my family treated me. My parents were awful to me. I had a younger sister named Kate and she was my best friend. She was the first one I came out to and she was always supportive of my happiness. She was the only one I introduced to my boyfriends. I didn't want my parents to find out for a long time because I didn't know what they would think. Eventually, Kate convinced me to tell them the truth because I was dating someone and thought he might be the one. I realized I wanted my parents to meet him, to be able to bring him to cookouts and holiday parties, family gatherings. I didn't want him to be a secret anymore and I think he was sick of it, too."

"So, you told them and it didn't go how you planned, right?" Edgar asked. "Like what happened when I told my parents?"

"Sort of. The difference is my dad was always violent, so when I told him I had a boyfriend and that I wanted to marry him, he lost it. He said, 'No son of mine will be with a man.' He started punching me as hard as he could. I think he was trying to kill me because he thought it was better if I was dead. Kate came home from school and found me lying on the bathroom floor with blood all over my face and stomach. One of my eyes was swollen shut and I could barely move. I was drifting in and out of consciousness and debating if I should let myself pass out and be done with it, but Kate called an ambulance and I was taken to the hospital."

"Then you left home?" Edgar asked.

Liam smiled somberly. "Not exactly. As soon as I was mostly healed, I left the hospital and went home during the middle of the night when I knew my parents were home. Kate was staying the night at a friend's house. I poured gasoline all over the house and lit a few matches, then ran outside to watch the house become engulfed in flames. The only regret I have is that I didn't make sure Kate was gone. She was supposed to be at her friend's house, but she had a migraine, so she canceled at the last minute and stayed home. She didn't make it out of the fire."

"What about your parents?"

"They died too, but they deserved it. Kate didn't," Liam said, struggling to finish the sentence.

Edgar tilted his head to the side, sizing up Liam. "Let's keep hiking," was all he said as he stood from the boulder, grabbed the bag with their snacks, and started climbing the trail again. Liam followed Edgar until they reached the top where there was a giant waterfall and open water for swimming. The area near the waterfall had a chain-link fence around it to stop people from falling, but the fence clearly wasn't well maintained because there was a large gap in it. No one else was on the trail or near the waterfall.

"Stand in front of the fence," Edgar said, pulling out his phone. "I'll take a picture of you and then we can take one together."

"Okay," Liam agreed, moving towards the waterfall to stand in front of the chain-link fence. He grinned widely as he waited for Edgar to take the picture.

Edgar joined Liam by the waterfall and turned to him. "You're right, by the way. I think I do love you," Edgar said.

Liam grinned. Edgar wrapped his arms around Liam in what he first interpreted as a hug until he realized Edgar was squeezing him as hard as he could and he tried to pull away. Edgar shoved Liam towards the opening in the fence. There was loose soil around the fence and Liam's foot slipped as he tried to regain his balance. Edgar seized the opportunity and pushed Liam in the chest just as Liam thought he was stable. Liam tried to grab Edgar's hand to pull himself to safety.

"Edgar, help!" Liam shrieked.

Edgar let Liam hold his hand one last time. "This is for the best. I can't have any weaknesses."

Edgar let go of Liam's hand and shoved him hard in the chest. Liam tried to grab something to hold onto and managed to grasp a piece of the fence, but it wasn't secure and not meant to hold anyone's weight, so a piece of it tore off in his hands, and he tumbled through the air screaming.

Jackson appeared beside Edgar, shaking his blood-soaked head in disapproval. "Edgar, you can't go around killing anyone you want to. Why do you do this? Despite your craziness, he loved you and I thought you loved him too."

"Stop it!" Edgar yelled. "I didn't ask for your opinion, Jackson. You don't understand. I'm incapable of love."

Jackson hovered beside Edgar as he leaned over the fence to watch Liam tumble through the air and into the roaring waterfall. Even if Liam was a decent swimmer, the current was too strong. He wouldn't be able to fight against the current and make it to land. As Liam fell, Edgar stared into his eyes, seeing the look of complete and utter betrayal.

# Chapter 22: Delia

Delia and Jerry checked into their hotel; they only booked one hotel room because there were two queen-sized beds in the room and it was much cheaper than paying for two rooms. Besides, Delia dragged Jerry back into the case and would have felt guilty if he was forced to pay for his own room, on top of all the other required expenses for the trip. They were both starving after a long day of travel and lack of food, so after Googling restaurants in the area, they stumbled across a tempting option. In downtown Minneapolis, there was a restaurant called Annie's Parlour, known for their ice cream and burgers, with rooftop seating overlooking the bustling city. The frigid air and dropping temperatures as evening approached made it less desirable to eat outside.

Ever since they landed in Minneapolis, Delia hoped she would run into Prince. She knew it was probably futile, but she wondered what the King of Purple was doing and if he was out and about in Minneapolis at the moment.

"What's the plan of attack?" Jerry asked Delia when they were seated at Annie's and waiting for their food.

Delia paused thoughtfully. "I've been researching Edgar and found his parent's last known address. They moved there over 30 years ago and Edgar grew up there, so I thought he would go to his parent's house if he wanted a safe place to retreat. It's in downtown Minneapolis, pretty close by actually, so I thought we could drop by the house after we eat and see if anyone is home. If Edgar isn't there, then I hope we can obtain a lead from his parents. Even if he isn't staying with them, I'm sure they know where he is."

Jerry nodded. "Sounds good. Wouldn't it be great if Liam was there with Edgar too? We could nab 'em both in one go."

Delia smiled. "We can only hope it will work out that way."

Jerry's phone rang as he was about to reply to Delia. "Sorry, I better take this outside. I'll be back in a minute."

While Jerry was outside, the waitress brought their food over. Delia and Jerry had both ordered burgers and fries, but Delia opted for a chocolate shake, while Jerry chose strawberry. Delia's stomach grumbled, but she politely waited for Jerry to return before she began eating.

"Holy smokes," Jerry said as he returned and sat down across from Delia in the booth.

"What's up?" Delia asked, immediately shoveling a few French fries into her mouth.

"It was my friend in Mexico again. He did some more digging on Liam and discovered something interesting. Liam's car was left at an auto repair shop in Shawnee, Oklahoma. The local police looked up the license plate number and found out it was registered to Liam. But, that's not the weirdest part."

"What?" Delia asked, sipping her chocolate shake and leaning forward.

"The owner of the auto repair shop was found dead in the garage of his shop at the beginning of the week. The police couldn't find a weapon, but he appeared to be bludgeoned to death with a club or some sort of tool. There was a nasty gouge in his head from where he was struck multiple times. An employee discovered him after it happened, but there weren't any witnesses. However, the employee described two men who looked to be in their thirties traveling together. They showed up at the shop the previous day. His descriptions are in line with Edgar and Liam's appearances."

Delia grinned, folding her arms and leaning back against the vinyl booth. "We've got them. If they killed that mechanic, that's it. It's over."

"The problem is there weren't any fingerprints at the crime scene and the weapon used to kill the mechanic was never found."

Delia sat up straight in the booth, remembering the tragic story she saw on the news at the beginning of the week. "Wait. I watched the news on Monday or Tuesday and saw a story about a mechanic who was found dead in his auto repair shop in Oklahoma. It must have been the same man," she said excitedly.

Jerry nodded slowly. "It would be quite a coincidence if the mechanic's murder is connected to Edgar and Liam. This might be easier than we thought. But, enough work talk, let's enjoy our dinner and pay Edgar's parents a nice little visit afterwards."

"I agree," Delia said, taking a large bite of her cheeseburger. "This place is fantastic. I'm glad we found it."

Jerry took his first bite of his bacon cheeseburger. "As a New Yorker and self-proclaimed food snob, I have to admit I didn't know food could taste this good in the Midwest."

Delia and Jerry finished their dinner at Annie's and headed towards Edgar's parent's house, which was only a few blocks away from the restaurant. As they walked, the blistery, Midwestern air howled around them. Delia shivered as they walked across the pedestrian path on the Stone Arch Bridge and wished she brought warmer gloves, as the icy air bit through the thin fleece. She shoved her hands into her coat pocket for more warmth and trudged on.

When they arrived at the address listed as Barbara and Jerald Peterson's house, they stopped on the driveway.

"Are you ready?" Jerry asked.

Delia nodded, this time not only shivering from the cold but also from nervous energy.

Delia and Jerry walked the last few steps to the front door and stood on the stairs. Delia rang the doorbell and Jerry smiled reassuringly at her as they waited for someone to answer.

The door swung open. A man who appeared to be in his thirties, wearing jeans and a long-sleeve gray t-shirt, with tousled dark brown hair to his shoulders and dark eyes, answered.

"Mom!" The man called out, turning around to yell into the house. "There are two people at the door!"

Delia's eyes widened. It was Edgar.

# Chapter 23: Delia

Delia and Jerry were ushered into Barbara and Jerald Peterson's house by Edgar, offered coffee by a jittery Barbara, and gathered in the living room.

Delia flashed her old police badge as a form of trusted ID to be let into the house. "My name is Delia Wilson. I'm a former police officer and Jerry is a private detective. We're visiting from New York and need to speak with your son."

"Oh dear," Barbara said, drinking her coffee, even though she already drank several cups and was only running on coffee and adrenaline. "Is there a problem?"

Delia was relieved Barbara didn't seem to gather that, technically, she and Jerry didn't have the legal authority to arrest anyone. She did her best to hide her relief.

"Unfortunately, ma'am, yes, there is a problem. I'm not sure how much your son has told you about the Jackson Birkman case—" Delia started, but was cut off by Barbara.

"Edgar was in an accident a few months ago and lost his memory. He doesn't remember anything before the accident," Barbara explained.

Delia's eyes narrowed and she turned to Edgar. "You don't remember *anything*?"

"Nope," Edgar said, assessing Delia and Jerry.

"So, you don't know who I am then?" Delia asked.

Edgar shrugged his shoulders. "No, sorry."

"I was one of the investigating officers on the Birkman case. I interrogated you while the case was ongoing," Delia said.

Barbara set down her coffee mug and crossed her arms over her large stomach. "Wasn't that case closed? I followed it on the news. Jackson's pretty little fiancée set the whole thing up. I think you two came all the way from New York for nothing."

Jerry cleared his throat. "Mrs. Peterson, we came to speak with your son. If he really lost his memory—"

Edgar stared blankly at Jerry and Delia.

Barbara cut off Jerry midsentence. "He doesn't remember a thing! He didn't even remember me when he first got here."

"How *did* you end up here, Edgar? And how did you find out where your parents lived?" Delia asked, whipping out her notepad and a pen, prepared to record the most obvious bullshit she's ever heard.

Edgar smiled, turning his dark eyes on Delia. "I was out with a friend in Lake Chapala and an American tourist couple recognized me. They wanted a picture with me because they recognized me from *Dispatching David*. I'm sure you saw it on the news. After finding out I was famous, I was able to do a few Google searches to find as much information as possible about my past. It's amazing what you can find out about a person online. I found my parent's last known address and hoped they were still living here. Then, I took a bus to Minneapolis from Lake Chapala."

A million questions bubbled inside of Delia's mind. She forced herself to take a deep breath before continuing the conversation. "Did you travel here alone? Who is your friend from Lake Chapala?" She asked, although she already knew Liam's name and was almost positive he traveled with Edgar.

"His name is Liam. He did come here with me, but he left yesterday."

"Where did he go?" Jerry asked.

Edgar rolled his eyes. "Back to Lake Chapala. His apartment, I'm assuming."

"What do you know about Liam?" Delia asked.

"What do you mean? I only knew him for a few months," Edgar responded.

"Are these questions necessary?" Barbara interjected. "Why are you interrogating him? He's been here with me all week. He hasn't done anything wrong," she insisted.

"Edgar was one of the suspects in the Birkman case—" Delia started.

"The case has been closed for months! Besides, it wasn't Edgar's fault. Jackson was his best friend. They were friends since they were toddlers. Edgar would never hurt him."

Delia turned to Edgar, disappointed. "You don't remember *anything* about the case?"

"The first thing I remember is waking up in Lake Chapala, exhausted, hungry, and confused. I wandered around the city until I found a restaurant with a bar. That's where I met Liam. He was the bartender there. But, no, I don't remember any details about the case or Jackson. I wish I could help more," Edgar said, standing from his spot on the couch next to Barbara.

"Well, it's been nice chatting with you both, but I think it's time for you to go," Barbara said swiftly, standing from the couch and ushering Delia and Jerry towards the front door.

Delia and Jerry conceded, setting down their untouched coffee mugs.

"If you remember any details about the case that could potentially be helpful, please give us a call," Delia said, handing Edgar one of her business cards.

"Alright," Edgar said with a small smile, glancing at the business card and slipping it into his pocket.

Delia and Jerry left the Peterson house. When they were in their rental car and Jerry backed the car out of the driveway, Delia finished scribbling her notes in her notepad and spoke.

"I don't believe him. I think he's lying about losing his memory because he knows we're on to him. He's terrified that after all this time he could still be convicted," Delia said, tapping her pen against the notepad.

"I don't know, Delia. He seemed confused. I'm not sure if he faked the memory loss," Jerry said.

"It didn't help that his mom interrupted the conversation every time we asked a question or when she thought Edgar was going to say something dangerous."

"Yeah, it would have been better if we had been alone with Edgar. I think he would have talked more if Barbara wasn't with him," Jerry admitted.

"Plus, how did Edgar lose his memory? He said the first thing he remembered was waking up in Lake Chapala, but how did he travel there? And why did he go to Mexico, of all places?" Delia wondered aloud.

"Those are all good questions. I could call my friend in Mexico again and ask him to look into where Edgar Peterson lived and worked, if he had any credit cards, rented or purchased a car, anything else to help us."

"Thanks, Jerry. The more we can find out, the better chance we have of ending this once and for all," Delia said. "Do you think he drove his own car to Mexico? You should ask your friend to look up Edgar's license plate number and search for his car. He said he took the bus to Minneapolis, so he clearly didn't bring it with him. Unless he lied about that too."

"Alright, I'll make a list of questions for my friend and give him a call when we're back at the hotel. You know what else I'm curious about?"

"What?"

"Why did Liam travel here with Edgar and leave after only spending a few days here? Do you think he only came along to make sure Edgar found his family? Or do you think…" Jerry trailed off, contemplating Edgar's motive and intentions.

"That he killed Liam? That's what I wondered as soon as Edgar said Liam went home. They must have been close if Liam traveled across an entire country for someone he only knew for a short time," Delia said thoughtfully.

"Do you think they were involved? Romantically, I mean?" Jerry asked.

"Edgar and Liam? I didn't think about it before, but I suppose… Wait a second!" Delia screamed.

Jerry slammed on the brakes when Delia yelled and was nearly rear-ended by the car behind them. "Fuck, Delia! Don't scream when I'm driving unless there's a kid or a puppy or something in the road!" Jerry accelerated once again.

"Sorry! I realized something and it might be a huge piece of the puzzle we've been missing. What you said about Edgar and Liam being romantically involved made me think about Edgar and Jackson's relationship. I always wondered what Edgar's true motive was for killing Jackson and Clara. If he loved Jackson, or some sort of sick, twisted obsession he mistook for love, then killing Jackson and his fiancée would make sense, right?"

"Damn. I wish you didn't have that realization while I was driving and nearly caused an accident. It would be great if your theory was right though. It would answer a lot of questions. If Edgar killed Liam, then maybe he's killing the people he loves. But that doesn't make sense. You don't kill the people you love. Besides, he didn't kill his mom," Jerry said, shaking his head.

"Maybe not, but where was his dad? There wasn't any sign of him when we were at the house. They didn't mention where he was. We should look into that too," Delia said.

"Okay, but I think you might be reaching a bit. We have no reason to suspect Edgar killed his dad and we don't know if Liam is dead either," Jerry responded, tightening his hands on the steering wheel as he came down from Delia's outburst. "I know you're all ready to lock him up, but we need proof before we can make that happen."

When they were back at the hotel, Jerry called his connection in Mexico and updated him on the situation. His friend said he would call Jerry back if he found out any information about where Edgar lived and worked in Mexico or what happened to his car.

Delia restlessly paced across the hotel room. She felt like they were close, but there was still so much left to figure out if they wanted to nab Edgar for all his crimes. She kept spinning around the idea of Edgar being in love with Jackson and framing Clara for his death. She liked the idea; it made sense, but how could she prove it when the case was closed months ago? The only incriminating evidence discovered was the paracord bracelet Delia had picked up from Jackson and Clara's apartment after Clara's death. She found it while investigating the crime scene by herself, although the police chief thought she could have planted it, and had confiscated the bracelet. The information Edgar revealed to Delia during interrogations had been regarding Jackson's secrets, his financial struggles, how he loaned Jackson money, and tried to bail him out of a tough situation. Edgar never confessed to the murders.

After hanging out in the hotel room all day going over the details of the case with Jerry and talking through every clue they thought was pertinent, Jerry received a phone call from Luis, his connection in Mexico. He had news, although not the news they were expecting.

"Delia, I have news," Jerry said, hanging up his cell phone and plopping down onto one of the queen-sized beds.

"Now what?" Delia asked.

"My buddy Luis already investigated the make and model of Edgar's car and the license plate number. It won't be easy to track down his car because we don't know what he did with it or where he left it. It could be in Mexico or he could have abandoned it on the way to Minneapolis if he lied about taking the bus, so that will probably take longer to figure out. We need to acquire a search warrant for the Peterson house to see if we can find evidence to connect Edgar and Liam to the mechanic's death in Shawnee, Oklahoma. If we can find the weapon or another piece of evidence that ties back to the case, then that's all we need."

"Will it be enough?" Delia asked. "I thought I had sufficient evidence when I worked on the Birkman case last year, but the police chief and other investigating officers didn't think so. I don't want a repeat of last time. I can't deal with the loss again. Edgar can't keep getting away with murder."

"He won't, Delia. Eventually, we will catch him. If it's not now, then soon," Jerry said.

"I know you're trying to comfort me, but I don't relish the idea of a murderer freely roaming the world and continuing to kill because he keeps slipping through our fingers."

"I don't like it either. This is the first time I've ever dealt with someone like this. It's an interesting case, which is why I was all too happy to work on it with you, but it's never easy to pin down a criminal…well, I wouldn't call him a criminal mastermind exactly, but you see my point."

"I know. I keep thinking about all the famous serial killers who got away with murder for years until they were finally captured. Ted Bundy. Jeffrey Dahmer. John Wayne Gacy."

"Those are all extreme cases, Delia. Serial killers aren't common. Besides, other than Jackson and Clara, we don't know if Edgar has killed anyone else, so we might not be dealing with a serial killer. Maybe the mechanic at the auto repair shop and Liam were killed by Edgar, but we don't have any evidence to support those theories yet," Jerry said.

"We will though. I know we will. We have to."

Delia and Jerry ordered room service for dinner and tried their best to obtain a search warrant for the Peterson house. Since Delia wasn't an active police officer anymore, she leveraged every connection she could with the Minneapolis police. Jerry was a private detective, so he was used to dealing with law enforcement not taking him seriously, acting as if he was an average citizen trying to solve cases. In reality, he was a highly trained individual who excelled at his job and had successfully solved a multitude of cases over the years. In the end, Jerry convinced the Minneapolis police chief that the search warrant was necessary. After hours of going over the case files, the evidence, and their suspicions, Jerry proved they had probable cause to search the Peterson house. The police chief agreed on the condition that they bring an experienced police officer named Bill with them to oversee their search in case Edgar resisted or attempted to flee. It was late into the night by the time they had the search warrant approved. Delia and Jerry thought waiting one more day wouldn't change the outcome, so they went to sleep with the plan to return to the Peterson house in the morning.

# Chapter 24: Edgar

After Delia and Jerry left, Barbara turned to Edgar. "Do you remember anything about Jackson's death and the investigation?" Barbara asked, anxiously scrubbing the coffee mugs in the kitchen sink.

"No. I don't remember much," Edgar said, handing his mom the last of the dirty coffee mugs. "But I know I killed him."

Barbara dropped the mug in her hand and it shattered on the linoleum floor, ceramic pieces flying across the room. Edgar jumped back so he wouldn't step on any shards of the mug.

"Wh-what?" Barbara said, ignoring the mess and staring at Edgar. "I don't believe you. He was your best friend."

"I've been having flashes of memory. I think they're real. I remember holding Jackson's body after he died. I remember shooting Clara in the head and setting up the scene, so it looked like a suicide and framing her for Jackson's death with a suicide note," Edgar said, looking directly at Barbara. "I remember how it felt to kill. Ever since then, I've been chasing that feeling. I want it back."

"Oh, Edgar," Barbara said, sobbing and grabbing the broom so she could sweep up the pieces of the coffee mug she broke. "Why did you do it? What on Earth made you want to kill him? He always looked out for you. He was the one who helped you obtain the role on *Dispatching David*. You always wanted to be an actor. I remember when you were a kid, you used to pretend to be other people. I think you liked being in someone else's shoes because you were overcome with so many dark thoughts. It was an escape if you were able to pretend to be someone else for a while."

Edgar pondered his mom's theory. "You might be right, Mom, but since I can't remember most of what happened or how I went free after committing those crimes, I'm not sure if Delia and Jerry have enough evidence to convict me. I'm assuming there wasn't enough evidence to point to me being the murderer when the case was open. If lazy police officers were involved, then deeming the case a suicide-homicide set up by Clara made the case a lot easier to wrap up because that would mean the person responsible was dead. However, if someone else set it up, which I'm assuming was me, then the case became more complicated."

Barbara finished sweeping and set the broom back in the closet. "Edgar, I don't know what happened to make you this way. I tried my best to raise you to be a morally upright person, but clearly—I failed somewhere along the way. I've done my best, but I can't keep cleaning up your messes forever."

Edgar smirked. "Okay. I'm sure you were the perfect parent and never screwed up. But what are you going to do? Turn me in to the police? You killed Dad, so you would go to prison too. I'll tell them what you did."

"I've been thinking about that and I don't believe I deserve to live anymore. I should be in prison for what I did and for helping you discard the animal carcasses for all those years. And for what you did to Eliot when you were a small child. I should have stopped it then. If you had gotten the help you needed, maybe it wouldn't have turned out this way. I'm so sorry, Edgar."

"No. I'm sorry, Mom," Edgar said, lunging to grab a knife from the knife block on the counter.

Barbara immediately grabbed a knife as well and ran to the other side of the kitchen. For being an overweight woman in her mid-sixties, she was still in surprisingly good shape.

Edgar and Barbara stared each other down, each holding a knife and daring the other person to strike first in some sort of bizarre mother-son showdown. Edgar was almost disappointed that after all they went through together, his mom betrayed him. He knew she didn't love him. She only felt guilt after finding out the extent of what he did and that he continued killing, even going so far as to kill his best friend. He didn't need to explain his reasoning to her. He didn't fully understand himself, but after killing Liam, he knew he wouldn't be able to find love and that was what made it so easy to jump forward and stab his mom in the stomach.

He wrenched the knife around, pulling it out and plunging it into her stomach again, where it stuck the second time. Barbara moaned and stumbled backwards, bumping into the counter as she struggled to free the knife from her stomach. She howled and managed to pull it out, but the damage was done. Barbara stabbed Edgar in the arm, attempting to gain control of the situation, although she was going to die from her knife wounds. Edgar knew she wanted to take him down before she died, but he wasn't going to let that happen.

Edgar plunged the knife into his mom's heart this time, knowing that aiming for a vital organ was his best bet to end the struggle quickly. Barbara clutched at her chest, gasping for breath and crying from the immense pain. Edgar drove the knife into his mom's chest a final time, watching as she realized it was over and slumped to the kitchen floor, closing her eyes in defeat.

Edgar clutched his left arm where it bled freely and tightly bandaged it using a wrap from the first aid kit in the hallway bathroom. He appraised the mess in the kitchen, looking at his mom's motionless body, the bloody knives, and the immense amount of blood on the linoleum floor and counter from where his mom fell. He had to clean up the mess by himself this time and figure out how to get rid of her body quickly. He wasn't sure if Delia and Jerry would return, but he suspected they would, especially considering they wouldn't let go of the case.

As Edgar poured bleach on the linoleum in an attempt to clean up the blood, the doorbell rang. He immediately sprinted to the spare bedroom where he slept the past few nights, tugged on his boots, and put on his coat as quickly as possible while trying to minimize the pain on his left arm. His mind raced as he contemplated where to go and what he should grab before leaving. He assumed he had at least a few minutes before they would try to break the lock on the door or find another way in. He wished he had more time to explore the house now that his mom was gone. Who knew what other secrets she kept from him?

The doorbell rang again. This time, a voice followed, "Edgar, Barbara, are you home? It's Delia Wilson. I have a search warrant for the house."

"Fuck," he muttered as he searched Barbara's bedroom for a gun. He had a hunch she was the type of woman who kept guns in the house. He wildly opened the closet door and ripped open the nightstand drawers. When he opened the bottom drawer of the nightstand, he sighed in relief as he spotted a Glock 26 buried beneath a stack of papers. It was a small 9 mm, perfect for concealed carry, and light enough for his mom to easily use it. He grabbed the magazines stashed next to it and loaded the gun. He needed to be ready.

A series of loud knocks sounded on the front door. "Edgar! Open up!" Delia yelled.

Edgar headed to the door to look through the peephole. He saw Delia, Jerry, and an unknown man in a police uniform on the doorstep. He wondered if he could overpower all three of them. It seemed unlikely. He knew his best bet was to leave the house and escape. He had gotten away with murder before and he didn't plan on going to prison this time.

He dashed to the door leading to the basement, thinking about how sad it was that things were ending this way. He traveled to Minnesota hoping his family would welcome him with open arms. Instead, he discovered his dad was dead and his mom was a murderer, just like him. Now she was dead, too. But he couldn't dwell on it. He needed to leave now.

Edgar descended the basement stairs two at a time, unlocking the sliding glass door in the basement's main room. He wouldn't be able to lock it behind him but maybe he could get a head start on them before they realized he left the house. As he opened the door, the air immediately chilled him. He zipped his coat all the way to his chin and hesitantly stepped into the fresh powdered snow in the backyard. It had been a cool spring day, but as evening descended the temperature dropped, and it was now below freezing. Snow began to come down faster. Edgar squinted into the yard, trying to determine the best path through the snow. They would see his footprints no matter which way he went.

"Well, fuck it. Let them find me and see what happens," he said to himself as he took off through the backyard, clutching the gun in his right hand.

He shivered in his thin coat as he tried his best to run through the steadily falling snow. His boots were a cheap pair from Target. They weren't insulated and weren't fit for walking through the snow. He wasn't prepared for the unpredictable Minneapolis weather. His socks and feet were soaked after several minutes. Edgar knew he couldn't survive outside in a snowstorm through the night. He needed a plan, but first he needed to find shelter somewhere safe.

# Chapter 25: Delia

Jerry pulled a few flashlights out of the glove compartment in the car. It would be dark soon and Edgar might have left the house already. Delia, Jerry, and Bill waited fifteen minutes on the front steps of the Peterson house, while ringing the doorbell and knocking on the door. They suspected Edgar either wasn't inside anymore or waiting for them to break into the house. The snow started coming down harder and they didn't want to wait any longer. They needed to act before Edgar escaped.

Jerry opened his bag and pulled out his lock pick set. Bill stared at him disapprovingly and Jerry smiled sheepishly as he opened the kit. Delia simply laughed, but covered her face with her hand when she noticed the look on Bill's face.

"I've been a private detective for years," Jerry said, picking up the tension wrench. "I wouldn't have made it this long if I didn't know how to pick a lock."

Jerry expertly pressed the wrench on the bottom of the lock and asked Delia to hand him the lock pick. He pushed down on the wrench, and inserted the pick, turning the tension wrench first to the left, then to the right when nothing happened. He distinctly heard the pins drop and victoriously opened the door after several more minutes of fiddling.

"After you," Jerry said graciously to Delia, but Bill stepped into the house first and cocked his 9 mm.

Bill surveyed the room, motioning silently for Jerry and Delia to follow him. They traipsed in after Bill, cautiously searching the room for any indication Edgar was there. They didn't find anything noteworthy and headed through the family room to begin searching the rest of the house.

Delia, Jerry, and Bill entered the kitchen and examined the area, each of them with varying degrees of horror on their faces as they saw Barbara's body lying on the kitchen floor in a puddle of blood mixed with bleach. The container of bleach sat half-empty next to Barbara's body, along with a rag and several kitchen knives drenched in blood. Delia immediately ran to her, noticing her ripped sweater covered in blood, presumably from being stabbed with a knife. She knelt by Barbara's side and checked her pulse, sighing loudly as she stood.

"Barbara Peterson is dead," Delia said solemnly, appraising the rest of the kitchen. "We need to find Edgar. He's probably fled by now."

Bill was already dialing 911. He shook his head as the phone rang. "We're following protocol. We had a search warrant for the house. Clearly, the situation has changed since we found a body, but it's dangerous to go after him, especially in this weather," he said, looking out the large kitchen windows to stare at what was becoming the storm of the century.

Jerry rubbed his mustache thoughtfully. "Let's finish searching the house first and see what we find. There could be evidence related to the Birkman case, or the mechanic's death, or Liam's disappearance."

Delia nodded. "Okay, fine. We'll do a quick search, then go after Edgar."

Delia and Jerry split up, searching different rooms simultaneously. Bill stayed in the kitchen by Barbara's body securing the crime scene. He needed to wait for the CSI unit to show up, document the crime scene, and collect any evidence.

Jerry called for Delia and she hurried into the master bedroom to find him by the nightstand.

"There is ammunition in here and the drawer was open," he stood, looking at Delia with a grim face. "I bet Edgar's armed."

"Okay. Well, we've searched almost every room and haven't found Edgar or any clues yet. The only room left is the basement," Delia replied.

Delia and Jerry had identical expressions of realization on their faces as they both recognized what that meant. Either Edgar was in the basement waiting for them or he had left the house through the basement door.

"Shit," Delia said. "One of us should have staked out the yard or the back door. What were we thinking?" She said in frustration as she exited the bedroom and thundered down the basement stairs.

"Delia, wait!" Jerry called, scrambling to follow Delia. "Don't run down there!"

Delia paused on the last step leading to the basement. If Edgar was down there, he would have heard her. "Edgar, are you here?"

There was no response. Jerry stopped next to Delia and they both continued into the basement, anxiously searching the room with their guns ready to fire.

"There's probably another room back there," Delia said, pointing to the hallway.

Delia and Jerry entered the small room off of the main area of the basement. Delia flicked on the light switch and looked around.

"It's a laundry room," she said, surveying the ancient washer and dryer and the large sink in the dimly lit room.

"No shit," Jerry replied, smiling good-naturedly at Delia. "Wait, what's in the sink?" Jerry asked.

Delia moved closer to the sink to inspect the inside. There was a clear jug on the counter. "Sulfuric acid?" She said in a confused tone after examining the label. "Why would the Petersons keep sulfuric acid in their laundry room? The jug is nearly empty."

Jerry sighed. "Well, it's not for anything good, that's for sure. We have a potential missing person and a nearly empty jug of sulfuric acid? Edgar might have used the acid to dissolve the body. Or at least most of it. I'm not sure if it would work for bones and teeth, but it could definitely erode skin."

Delia's face paled as she backed away from the sink and leaned against the wall, taking deep breaths to calm herself.

"Are you okay?" Jerry asked in concern.

"This is all my fault."

"No, it isn't. Besides, we can't be positive about the use for the sulfuric acid until we have proof," Jerry said unconvincingly. "Come on, Edgar isn't here, so we should search the perimeter of the house. I saw woods in the backyard. I bet that's where he went."

Delia straightened from her stance leaning against the wall and ran her hands through her curly red hair that was a tangled mess around her face. She grabbed an elastic from her wrist and wrapped it around her curls several times, tightening it so her unruly hair would stay in place. She looked at Jerry with resolve. "Let's go find Edgar."

# Chapter 26: Edgar

Edgar walked through the snowy woods for nearly twenty minutes, which seemed much longer due to his tired legs and soaked feet. He kept glancing over his shoulder back towards his parent's house, wondering when Delia, Jerry, and the policeman were going to catch up to him. He knew it was only a matter of time. He stopped for a moment to catch his breath, resting against one of the large oak trees nearby. The woods were full of trees over a hundred years old, their trunks standing proud and majestic, withstanding time. The branches were nearly naked and didn't provide much shelter from the rapidly cascading snowflakes. The snow drifts were higher than his knees now, making it harder for him to continue.

As Edgar leaned against the oak tree, the wind picked up, howling around him. The snow started falling even more ferociously. Edgar's legs felt shaky and he slumped down to the ground, wondering if he should give up. What was the point of running? He couldn't keep hiding forever. He suspected he wouldn't be able to escape from Delia again and wondered how he managed it the first time. He wished he could remember.

Edgar's eyelids felt heavy and he suddenly felt warm, despite the freezing temperature and snow falling harshly onto his exposed hands and face. Jackson appeared beside him, hovering above the snow.

"Edgar!" He yelled. "Snap out of it! You can't let them catch you. You've made it this far. I know you don't want to go to prison for the rest of your life."

Edgar's head snapped up as he saw Jackson. "Jackson! How do I get out of this mess?"

Jackson leaned closer to Edgar's face, the snow falling through his semi-translucent form, making his body eerily shimmer in the encroaching darkness. "You need to remember." Jackson's putrid scent made Edgar gag. "Remember what you did."

"What…did I…do?" Edgar asked slowly, his teeth chattering as the biting cold threatened to overtake him, looking at Jackson. "I know I—I killed…you."

Jackson smiled sadly. "But why?"

Edgar started to reply, but Jackson vanished before he could utter another word. "Jackson!" He screamed in anguish. "Jackson, please don't leave me again!"

Tears rolled down his cheeks. He was alone again. As Edgar tried to force his shaky legs upright, his memories came surging back to him in one blast. He gasped as his forgotten memories flowed through him and he was hit with a multitude of emotions. The fear of losing Jackson to Clara. The gut-wrenching agony of seeing Jackson and Clara together as the years passed. The turmoil that erupted through him when he decided to kill Jackson and the ensuing chaos. The glee and power surging through him when he killed Clara and her cat. Fleeing to Mexico to escape his past and start over. And finally, falling asleep at the wheel while he drove because he couldn't handle being alive anymore. Afterwards, he felt raw and tormented by what he remembered. But, at last he knew the truth. He did it all for love.

Edgar heard footsteps crunching through the snow. It sounded like several people coming towards him. He thought he was far enough away from his parent's house, but maybe he hadn't walked far at all. He didn't know how much time had passed. Edgar stared up at the sky as the inky darkness slowly stole the rest of the light. He attempted to run again, as fast as he could this time. But running was impossible because the snow was thicker and deeper now, so he trudged slowly through the snow. He didn't have a plan or any idea where he was headed, but he finally had his memories back.

"There he is! I see him!" Edgar heard a female voice yell as a flashlight shined on the tree by him. It was probably Delia, but it was difficult to tell because the voice was muffled from the howling wind and snow.

He heard a gunshot and instinctively ducked. "Shit!" Apparently, they weren't going to attempt to talk him down. He stopped running and turned to face the direction he thought the gunshot and the voice came from. Somehow, he managed to hold onto his mom's gun through all his running. He wiped the snow off of it and aimed into the blizzard.

Edgar heard a second gunshot closer this time and crouched down in the snow, rubbing his hands together in a weak attempt to warm them. He pushed his stringy dark hair from his face so he could see better, but it was futile. Night descended and the snowstorm made it impossible to see clearly. All he could make out were tiny white flakes falling around him. He could barely see a few feet in any direction.

He stood and fired off several shots, one after the other, aiming wildly. He was unsure if he was even facing the right direction until he heard a scream.

"Jerry!" The female voice yelled.

He smiled sadistically, assuming he hit his target. But that meant Delia would come after him for revenge.

A series of gunshots went off. Edgar felt one whiz by his ear and yelped. Another bullet grazed his right leg and he screamed in agony, using every ounce of strength left to remain standing. Blood dripped from the open wound on his torn pants into the snow. He fired his gun until he ran out of bullets and dropped the gun uselessly into the snow as Delia approached him, holding her gun down at her side, her curly red hair falling out of the elastic she used to try to keep it together.

Delia glared down at Edgar. He fell into the snow after dropping his gun.

"Are you ready to give up?" Delia asked, her chest heaving and her face covered in fresh tears.

Edgar tried to stand, but couldn't muster the strength. Delia sighed and extended her right hand to pull him up.

"You can lean against me. We're not very far from your parent's house. We can make it back there before the storm gets worse."

Edgar hesitated before accepting Delia's help, wondering if it was a trap, but decided he couldn't make it by himself. Edgar and Delia trudged through the snow together, his arm wrapped around her shoulders as she half-dragged him back to the house. Neither of them spoke as they walked; after a few minutes, they passed Jerry's body. He wasn't moving.

Edgar paused, looking at Delia. "Is he—?"

Delia cut him off before he could finish the question and dropped his arm from her shoulders. "Yes, you bastard!" She screamed, losing her thin semblance of control and violently striking him across the cheek.

They continued their journey back to the house in silence. This time, Delia walked slightly behind Edgar to make sure he wasn't going to attempt to flee. When they finally reached the Peterson house, Bill waited by the opening of the woods. He stared quizzically at Delia and then looked at Edgar.

"Where's Jerry?" Bill asked, his hands on his hips in a silly attempt to display his power.

"In the woods. We will need several people to carry his body back," Delia said quietly, a few tears betraying her and sliding down her cheeks.

Edgar smirked and Delia raised her hand as if she was going to smack him again, but thought better of it this time. There was a witness, after all.

Bill cleared his throat and pulled a pair of handcuffs from his belt. "Edgar Peterson, you are under arrest for the murders of Jackson Birkman, Clara Rogers, Jerry—"

"I get it, I get it," Edgar said, annoyed. "Just arrest me already."

Delia nodded and grabbed Edgar, holding his arms back as Bill handcuffed Edgar's hands. Edgar winced from his left arm being pulled back.

"You aren't getting away with it this time," Delia sneered. "You're going to pay for what you did."

Despite the intense amount of pain he was in, Edgar laughed loudly. "I have no intention of spending the rest of my life in prison. You have no idea what you just did."

# Chapter 27: Delia

Edgar awaited trial for the murders. Delia found the wrench used to kill the mechanic in the basement of Edgar's parent's house, as well as sulfuric acid in the large sink in the laundry room. Forensics also discovered traces of Jerald Peterson's DNA in the laundry room sink, but that could have been for any number of reasons. It was his house, after all. Delia hypothesized Edgar may have dissolved the bodies of his dad and Liam, but the investigation was ongoing. They didn't have any evidence of Liam's or Jerald's deaths. The missing bodies meant there were still mysteries left to be solved.

Unfortunately, Luis, Jerry's connection in Mexico, was unable to find Edgar's car and couldn't track down Liam, so a missing person's report was filed for Liam. Delia suspected Edgar killed Liam and disposed of the body and had most likely done the same for his dad, so she didn't know if they would be able to convict Edgar for those murders. However, since there was overwhelming evidence that Edgar killed his mom and the mechanic, it was enough for him to go to the Ramsey County Jail until the court disposition.

Jerry died almost immediately after Edgar shot him. Delia knew she would have to mourn his death eventually, but for now she focused on Edgar. It was going to be an uphill battle until she was certain Edgar would spend the rest of his life behind bars, but it was a battle she was willing to fight. She didn't want Jerry to have died in vain. It was her fault for dragging him into the mess with Edgar. Delia knew the risks going into it, but blamed herself for not being able to face it alone.

Delia planned to start her own detective agency when she was back in New York. With her mom and Jerry both gone now, the only people she had left were Becca and Joel. She supposed if she wanted to start her own agency, she would need to find a partner or at the very least she would need to hire someone she could train to work with her on cases. For now, she planned to stay in Minneapolis until she knew the outcome of Edgar's court disposition.

Delia visited the jail where Edgar was temporarily detained nearly every day. Edgar refused to speak to her and denied any involvement in the deaths and missing people when interrogated. He claimed to not know where Liam was and insisted his dad died from lung cancer. Delia still wondered if he was faking the memory loss or if he really didn't remember what happened. She supposed it didn't matter. At this point, she felt positive that the Minneapolis Police Department and the judge overseeing Edgar's trial would make the right decision.

Delia entered the jail for the third time in a week and stood outside of Edgar's cell. Delia smiled at him.

"Hello, Edgar," she said, assuming he wouldn't reply. She held out hope that he would confess to murdering Jackson and Clara, so he could be tried for those homicides as well.

Edgar peered through the bars of the cell, gripping them so tightly his knuckles turned white. His long, straggly hair hung around his face, but he brushed it away to see more clearly. Edgar's dark eyes bore into Delia for a long moment. His voice was vicious when he finally spoke. "Hello, Delia," he said, a maniacal smile spreading across his face. "You will pay."

## Note from the Author

Dear Reader,

I would like to thank you for purchasing my book. I hope you enjoyed the mystery and that you were on the edge of your seat trying to find out what was going to happen to Edgar and Delia.

Please consider taking a few minutes to write an honest review for *The Long Shadow of Memory* on Goodreads and the website where you purchased the book. Reviews are so important for indie authors because it helps readers determine which books to buy. If you would like to help spread the word about *The Long Shadow of Memory*, please leave a review!

Thank you so much for your support!

# Acknowledgements

As always, I would like to thank my extraordinarily wonderful husband, Zed, for his daily support and encouragement to pursue my dreams. He's so understanding and patient when I spend many of my nights and weekends writing, editing, marketing, and everything else that is involved in being an author. I couldn't do this without him.

Next, I owe a huge thank you to Alex Noelke, the editor of both of my books. He provided suggestions for improvements, pointed out plot holes and inconsistencies, cut awkward wording, and so much more that I can't even begin to name it all.

I'm thankful to have remarkably supportive parents who never doubted I would be an author. They're my biggest fans and at least a few of my book sales are a result of them telling people about my books.

I'm also incredibly grateful to have awesome beta readers. Jessica Skinner, Kate Postma, and Robert Hayek, thank you so much for reading *The Long Shadow of Memory* while I was still trying to figure out where the story was going. Your insight as readers was instrumental in shaping the final manuscript.

A few other people I would like to thank are Heather McKenzie, Alicia Kent, and Kaylee Koslowske. They are an essential part of my support system.

Lastly, thank you to my readers for buying my books, telling your friends and family about them, posting reviews on social media, sharing my posts, and loving thrillers like I do.